1 9/25 $2.00

Carols and Crimes, Gifts and Grifters

An anthology of holiday crime stories to
benefit the Toys for Tots

Compiled and edited by
Tony Burton

These stories are works of fiction. Names, characters, places and incidents are either the product of the authors' imaginations or are used fictitiously, and any resemblance to actual persons, living or dead, business establishments, events or locales is entirely coincidental.

Carols and Crimes, Gifts and Grifters

First printing – September 2007
Wolfmont Publishing,
Copyright ©2007 Wolfmont Publishing
All Rights Reserved
ISBN 978-1-60364-002-2

This book may not be reproduced in whole or in part, by mimeograph, photocopy, or any other means, electronic or physical, without express written permission of the copyright holders. The individual stories are copyrighted to their respective authors.

For information, contact:
info@wolfmont.com
or
Wolfmont Publishing
PO Box 205
Ranger, GA 30734

Cover Design by Tony Burton

Table of Contents

Ho Ho Homicide 1
Robbery on Christmas Eve......................... 19
The Lesson of the Season.......................... 37
Santa and the Poor Box 53
The Proper Trimmings 69
The Grinch And I 75
Home for Christmas 87
The Christmas Tree Thief 109
A Piece of Christmas............................... 131
Santa Solves A Murder 147
Mystery on Capitol Street 169
The Christmas Cutout Caper................... 187
Ballet Exercises....................................... 207
Christmas Every Day 213
Have a Harpy Christmas 223
Author Profiles.. 245

Ho Ho Homicide

An Odelia Grey Short Story

Sue Ann Jaffarian

Suddenly, my life had become a John le Carré novel.

Directly behind me was a woman with a gun. Ahead of me, near the end of the mall service corridor, was a man wearing a long dark trench coat and a fedora tilted slightly over one eye. He had a thick black beard and leaned against the wall next to a *No Smoking* sign. Clenched between his teeth was a lit cigarette.

"Bring her here," he ordered for the second time in a voice heavy with an Eastern European accent.

The woman poked the gun harder and deeper into my plus-size flesh. I remained still, frozen to the floor as if wearing cement overshoes. Dangling from each of my hands were several large and very heavy shopping bags. My mind raced with only two issues: 1) how did I get into this jam? and 2) how do I get out of it without getting my Christmas goose cooked?

The answer to my first question was easy. It's all Santa's fault. That's right, I'm laying this whole mess at the black-booted feet of Santa Claus. None of this would have happened if Santa hadn't sat his big fat red velvet behind next to my big fat denim-clad behind.

With only five shopping days left till Christmas, I, Odelia Patience Grey, found myself at Friendship Mall, the state of the art mall in Las Piernas, California. The place was mobbed with people, most with eyes of glazed frenzy, as they tried to finish their shopping on this last weekend before the big day. Having finished my Christmas shopping weeks ago, there was no good reason for my being here except that I was being held hostage by a peace-on-earth, goodwill toward men mentality that had outlived its usefulness by one day. Meaning yesterday, when my father called and begged me to take my crazy stepmother shopping as a favor to him, I should have said bah humbug and hung up.

But I love my Dad and it was Christmas. Even when he announced that Gigi wanted me to drive all the way to their house, pick her up and drive her all the way to Las Piernas to go to Friendship Mall, I didn't waiver in my commitment to holiday good cheer.

That was yesterday.

Today I'd had to listen to Gigi's endless prattle. She had talked non-stop the entire forty-five minute drive to the mall, the entire twenty minutes it had taken us to find a parking spot, and the entire time I escorted her from one packed store to another. Even stopping for lunch had not slowed down her mouth or her criticism of me one iota. The highlight of lunch was when Gigi tipped her bowl of soup. It splashed across the table and into my lap like a fast-moving lava flow. After lunch, I'd had to make a quick emergency stop at Lane Bryant to purchase a new pair of jeans and panties. As I left the store, a small child pushing a stroller plowed into the back of my legs and about severed the Achilles tendon on my right foot. Well, okay, not really severed it, but the assault was enough to make me yelp in pain and to draw blood.

The Ghost of Christmas Miserable had obviously decided to pay me a visit.

After telling Gigi she'd have to continue shopping without me, I hobbled to a bench and sat down. Injured foot aside, I considered the stroller incident a blessing. It bought me time alone and a chance to sit down for a while. At least until Santa plopped his big butt down next to me with all the grace of an elephant dancing the Nutcracker.

I glanced over at my new bench buddy, trying hard not to scowl as his shoulder knocked into mine. It was then that I noted that his Santa suit was grimy and tattered. Spying an empty bench a few yards away, I decided to move before he asked me to sit on his knee. I was in the midst of picking up my purse and shopping bag with my soiled clothing when the grubby Santa grabbed my arm.

Whipping my head around, I found

myself face to face with him. His dirty beard had slipped, uncovering thin pale lips. He blinked slowly but said nothing. He blinked again and tightened his grip on me. Without a sound, his lips squeezed together until all the blood drained from them. I thought at first he was drunk, but there was no smell of alcohol.

I tried to pry his fingers from my arm while he continued to blink and stare. Just as I was about to call out for help, he spoke.

"Help me." The two words were barely audible, but filled with fear.

I stopped trying to get away from him. "Are you ill?"

With his other arm, he reached around in front like he was making a grab at me but only succeeded in banging into my shopping bag as he slumped against me. I tried to disentangle his hand from the bag while supporting him, but didn't have much luck. Finally, his body shuddered a few times and went still.

"Are you ill?" I asked again.

I couldn't reach my cell phone so I shouted out to people walking nearby. "Call 9-1-1." Most ignored me and kept walking. Others stared but kept walking. A few stood frozen to the floor and stared slack-jawed.

I made eye contact with a man carrying a Gap bag. "You," I barked. "Call 9-1-1." My order surprised him but he did as I asked. "This man is ill," I continued, keeping the shopper locked in my sight as he punched numbers on his cell phone. "Get an ambulance."

A young woman in jeans and a sweatshirt pushed her way through the small crowd that had formed. "I'm a doctor," she announced.

The doctor squatted in front of Santa while I held him with one arm around him from behind and the other held against his chest. She checked his pulse then began working her hands quickly around his torso.

"Shouldn't we remove his coat?" I asked her.

She ignored me as her hands traveled up and down his legs, including between them. It looked more like a frisk job than an examination.

I was about to question her doctoring methods when the crowd stepped closer. I freed one of my hands and held it up. "Stay back. Give him some room."

Just then a woman in the group let out a little scream. Another scream followed. Everyone stared at me as if I were insane. Some scuttled away. The doctor disappeared as another woman screamed, this one louder than all the rest. I turned toward the scream and saw Gigi standing on the far right of the crowd, her hands slapped against both sides of her face in horror.

"Odelia, what have you done now?"

It was then that I noticed that the hand I was holding out to the crowd was covered with blood.

**

"How do you know Leon Weinberg?"

The man questioning me was a detective with the Las Piernas police who'd been called by mall security. He had introduced himself as Detective Aidan Wong. Standing alert but silent in a corner was a city cop. Seated at the far end of the table fidgeting with an unlit cigarette was Gigi. We were in a small conference room in the mall security office. The questioning had been going on for nearly an hour. It had been almost two hours since Santa expired in my arms.

"Who's Leon Weinberg?" I asked in return.

"The dead Santa."

"Santa's Jewish?"

The detective studied me over the top of his wire framed glasses. "Why not? At least he wouldn't mind working on Christmas."

"He's not the usual mall Santa, is he?"

"I'm supposed to be asking the questions here, Ms. Grey."

"Well," I continued, ignoring his comment, "seems to me that mall Santas are a bit more photogenic. This one was dirty and had a ragged beard. He was also on the second floor, not on the first floor where Santa usually sits in these places."

I was about to say more when Gigi interrupted. "How much longer you gonna be?" she demanded, looking from me to

Wong. "It's getting late and I have more shopping to do. I still don't have a thing for DeeDee's girls." As she spoke, her beehive hairdo, dyed remarkably like Pepto Bismol, nodded in time to her words.

Detective Wong started to say something, but I stopped him. "I'll handle this," I told him. "Believe me, you don't want to get involved."

Gigi looked hard at the detective. "I'm just her stepmother, ya know? She's no blood of mine." As she ranted, she shook the unlit cigarette like a symphony conductor's baton. "Takes after her no-good run-off mother, this one does. My kids would never do such a thing."

Detective Wong and I exchanged looks, then he said to me, "Be my guest."

I turned to Gigi. "Did you bring your cell phone?"

She pursed her lips in disapproval, but nodded.

"Please turn it on and go shopping. When you're done, just call me and I'll find you and we'll go home." I paused. "In fact, why don't you leave your packages and I'll take them to the car when I'm done here. That way you won't have to lug them around."

"Don't know why you can't stay out of trouble like normal people." Gigi was still mumbling about my shortcomings as she was led by a woman with mall security back to the shopping area.

I heard a throat clear and turned my attention back to Detective Wong.

"So, how do you know Leon Weinberg?" he asked again.

"I don't know Leon Weinberg," I insisted. "The man sat down next to me on the bench and two minutes later he was dead."

"Just like that?" He snapped his fingers.

"Yes, just like that." I resisted the urge to snap my fingers back at him. Instead, I turned one of my legs so he could see the gouge in my ankle. "I was the victim of hit-and-run stroller rage. See? Then I sat down on the bench to rest and along came Santa … um … Mr. Weinberg."

"You didn't know he'd been shot?"

"As I told you before, I knew nothing until I saw blood on my hands. Just before he collapsed, he asked me to help him. He never said how or why."

"And this woman, this doctor, you said she examined him and left."

"She claimed she was a doctor. But she more or less frisked him then took off." I paused. "Should I be calling my lawyer?"

Detective Wong knitted his brows in my direction. "I don't know, Ms. Grey; should you?"

I had done nothing wrong except sit my butt down on a bench to rest, but still, maybe having someone here to help me through the questions would help. But who? Seth Washington, lawyer and hubby of my best friend, Zee, was out of town. That left two people who could advise me: my boss, Michael Steele, a crackerjack corporate attorney and royal pain in my butt, and Detective Devon Frye of the Newport Beach police. Dev had already bailed me out of more pickles than I care to say. The choice was between enduring Steele's obnoxious remarks and Dev's stern admonitions to keep out of trouble. It was a tough call.

I looked up at Detective Wong. "May I have my cell phone? I'd like to call Detective Devon Frye of the Newport Beach police. He's a friend." Upon arrival, the police had confiscated my tote bag and the bag containing my soiled clothing. They had searched both, including Gigi's bags, which had set her off like a Fourth of July rocket.

"Dev Frye is a friend of yours?" There was disbelief in the good detective's voice.

I nodded.

"Then why don't I call him for you?" Detective Wong produced his own phone.

"The number is 949-555-8297," I said, trying to being helpful. "That's his direct line."

Detective Wong shot me a stern look as he punched in the numbers. He didn't have to wait long before his call was answered. "Hey, Dev. Aidan Wong in Las Piernas here." A pause. "Doing fine, thanks. Same ole', same ole. You know how it is." Another pause. "The reason I'm calling is I have someone here who says she's a friend of yours. An Odella Grey."

"That's Odelia," I corrected.

Detective Wong's look changed from stern to a mild scowl before he turned his back to me and lowered his voice. I strained to hear his end of the conversation, not doubting for a minute that Dev was giving him an earful of my colorful past with corpses.

"That was her?" Detective Wong turned around and openly stared at me while he listened to Dev. "Uh huh. I see." He held the phone out to me. There was an odd look on his face, like a smirk that was too pooped to complete the task. "He wants to speak with you."

My first inclination was to refuse the call, but I knew that would be a stupid thing to do. After all, I wanted Dev to help me, not to tell Wong to lock me up and throw away the key. I took the phone.

"Hi. Dev? I know this looks a tad odd, but I could really use your help." I was gripped by the babble gods and powerless to stop. "You see, all I did was sit down on a bench and Santa, well not the real Santa, sat next to me and died. I swear I had nothing, absolutely nothing to do with it and I have no idea who this person is … was. And I promise I …" Dev stopped me mid-sentence. I listened to him a few minutes, smart enough now to keep my mouth shut. When he was through, I handed the phone back to Detective Wong.

"Here," I said. "Your turn again."
***

Shortly after the call to Dev, I found myself back out in the mall loaded down with shopping bags. Detective Wong had told me to collect Gigi and to go home. Pronto. Under no circumstances was I to play detective in his city. His warning was also word-for-word what Dev had ordered me to do. They could have saved their breath. A pack of angry elves riding rabid reindeer could not have gotten me involved with Santa's murder. All I wanted was to find Gigi, drop her off at her house and head home to a hot bath and Chinese take out.

I made my way through the throngs of holiday decorations and crazed shoppers toward the exit nearest my car. My plan was to drop off the shopping bags then head back in to find Gigi. I'd called her cell phone but got no answer. She probably couldn't hear it with it stuffed in her handbag.

I was almost to the exit when someone bumped into me hard. I stumbled a bit but didn't fall, but I did lose my grip on the large shopping bags. They dropped to the ground in piles around me. Before I could dust myself off and gather up the bags, I was shoved again. This time I went down to my knees. Two people asked if I was alright. Someone else hooked a hand under one of my arms to help me to my feet.

I turned to thank my Good Samaritan only to find myself face to face with the woman who'd claimed to be a doctor. At the same time, I noticed that she had my arm in a death grip and was sticking something hard into my ribs with her other hand. I couldn't see what it was, but past experience told me it wasn't an umbrella.

She leaned in close. "Pick up the bags and get moving. Back that way."

The direction she was indicating wasn't out the door but back into the stream of shoppers. In a way, I was relieved. In spite of the gun, I felt safer inside. At least if she shot me, there would be witnesses. But then I remembered, no witnesses had come forward when Santa was shot.

"Did you kill Mr. Weinberg?"

She gave me a little shove. "Get moving, I said. And don't try anything funny. Just act normal."

I almost took the time to explain to her that having a gun jabbed into your ribs was in no way, shape or form normal. But then again, neither is a Jewish Santa being shot at the mall. So I buttoned my lip, picked up my shopping bags, and moved in the direction she'd indicated.

We were walking as fast as the crowd would allow. The woman stayed to my left just a footstep behind me and directed me by poking the gun to the left or right as if I were a horse guided by kicks. Soon we were near where the real mall Santa held court and the woman directed me to the right towards the service corridor which housed the restrooms and maintenance area. Fear settled in the pit of my stomach like bad sushi. I should be home decorating my Christmas tree and getting drunk on spiked eggnog, not being led to possible slaughter.

As we entered the long empty corridor, I spotted the man in the trench coat and fedora.

I took a tiny step, then another. It was a hesitant two-step that just might land me alongside Santa in the County Morgue, or it might buy me time to think through a plan of escape. We were close to him now. My nose tingled as it took in the smell of his smoke.

"There's no smoking," I told him.

He removed the cigarette from his lips and studied it with a slow half smile. "You Americans are so intolerant when it comes to tobacco." He leaned closer. "So what did you tell the police?"

"About what?"

"Do not play games. I do not like such things. Did Weinberg give you the merchandise?"

"You mean the dead Santa?"

The spy who came in from the mall held the lit cigarette under my nose. I could feel the heat close to my nostrils and began to worry that he was going to shove it up inside one.

"Like I told the police, I didn't know Mr. Weinberg."

"You expect me to believe that Weinberg simply sat down next to you, a complete stranger, and died?" He snapped his fingers as Detective Wong had. "Just like that?" For the second time that day, I found snapping fingers to be annoying. Had I not been carrying shopping bags, this time I would have snapped back, gun or no gun, cigarette or no cigarette.

"Just like that," I replied without the desired snap. I locked eyes with the man. "I guess he didn't want to die alone."

He held the cigarette a bit closer and I braced myself for the burn. After a few seconds, the creep withdrew it. Taking a few steps back, he flicked ash to the floor, stuck it back between his lips and took a long drag. As he exhaled, he stubbed the butt out on the *No Smoking* sign.

Keeping my eyes on the man in front of me, I strained my ears for sounds of other people, hoping someone would be either going in or out of one of the nearby restrooms. But all was silent. Didn't people in Las Piernas need to pee? Then I had second thoughts. There was a gun in my back. Dollars to donuts the thug in front of me had one also. Suddenly, the last thing I wanted was some unsuspecting holiday shopper stumbling upon this little gathering.

"One more time," the man said. "Where is the merchandise from Weinberg?"

He jerked his chin and the woman behind me pressed the gun deeper into my back, forcing me to move closer to him. My knees threatened to buckle and I could feel perspiration pooling under my arms, but I forced myself to stand still and continue the eye contact.

"The merchandise?" he prompted again.

In silence, I held out the Lane Bryant bag to him. He took it and rummaged through my dirty clothing until he extracted something of interest. He smiled at me. Maybe he got off on dirty granny panties.

"Excellent," he said as he held up a small velvet pouch in triumph.

Opening it, he dumped the contents into the palm of his hand. Out poured three huge diamonds, bigger than any I'd ever seen in my life. The fluorescent light in the corridor danced merrily on their facets as the creep displayed them. Geez, why hadn't the cops found those?

"Did you and Weinberg really think you would get away with this?"

Wide-eyed, I shook my head. "I had no idea those were in there. Truly."

He laughed and jerked his chin again to the woman behind me. "Take care of her."

The gun left my back. I had no idea where it was and I didn't want to know.

"Not here, you fool," he snapped. "Take her into one of the toilets."

Quickly, I analyzed the situation. Even though the woman was much younger and probably stronger, she was half my size. If I could disarm her in the bathroom, I might be able to strong arm her enough to save my neck. But the minute I tried to leave, the guy would easily take me down. He might even come in after me.

The gun was back in its place, prodding me to move towards the restroom. The man had forgotten me, focused instead on admiring his treasure. If I was to have half a chance, I was going to have to make a move right here. Right now.

Without warning, the door leading from the mall banged open and a custodian wheeling a maintenance cart of cleaning supplies entered the corridor. In the split second of surprise, I grabbed the remaining shopping bags with both hands and swung them with all my might in a wide circle. I struck the woman first, knocking the gun from her hand, and followed up and through into the head of the man as he reached for his own gun. The second impact caused the handles on the heavy bags to break, launching them out of my grip. I didn't know what Gigi had purchased, but I was thankful it wasn't bags of socks.

I took off down the corridor in the direction of the custodian, who to my surprise was holding a gun.

"Police, freeze!"

I froze.

***

Once again I found myself seated in the conference room of the Friendship Mall

Security Office. But this time I was a guest, not a detainee. Apparently, Detective Wong and his men had found the diamonds when they searched my bags earlier and left them there, hoping I would lead them to the real murderers.

Leon Weinberg, it turned out, wasn't Santa after all, but had been a career jewel thief. He had stolen the three spectacular diamonds from a master diamond cutter, who also had Russian mob connections. The two goons who killed him and grabbed me had been part of the retrieval team.

"You used Odelia as bait?" The question was directed at Detective Wong by Dev Frye. Sure I wouldn't be able to keep out of trouble, Dev had driven to Las Piernas as soon as he had hung up from our earlier call. Good man.

"It worked, didn't it?" Detective Wong smirked at his colleague from Newport Beach.

A moment later, Dev escorted me to the door. Looking back over my shoulder, I saw that Aidan Wong was still sprawled on the floor, blood running from his mouth.

Something told me all he'd want for Christmas would be his two front teeth.

Copyright ©2007 Sue Ann Jaffarian

Robbery on Christmas Eve
Earl Staggs

A little girl with red pigtails hugged Sheriff Mollie Goodall's leg and chanted, "Me nex, Shehwuff Mahwee, me nex."

Mollie looked down and smiled. "Yes, Courtney, you're next."

Wide-eyed, anxious little ones surrounded her, pushing and crowding forward for their turn to visit with Santa Claus. Behind her, the church's large Community Hall buzzed with the festive chatter of families enjoying their dinner. Mollie estimated some two hundred adults and, it seemed, twice that many children. Still, a loneliness tugged at her. Christmas Eve had always been a special time for her and her husband, but Lilburn was stranded in the Chicago airport due to a blizzard. Instead of going home to an empty house. Mollie had stopped by the church to help with the Christmas Eve party.

When her turn came, Mollie lifted Courtney and stepped onto the platform where Santa waited. "Here you go, sweetie. Tell Santa what you want for Christmas." Charlie Wickles played Santa, as he had for the last ten years. Charlie was perfect for the job. His white beard was real, his "Ho, Ho, Ho" was perfect, and he needed no padding for the Santa suit.

Mollie turned to step off the platform and saw Pastor Jimmy Wilson making his way across the room toward her. He ignored those who spoke to him, which was unusual for him, and held a grim expression on his face, which was also unusual for the normally jovial man.

He reached her side, leaned close, and whispered, "It's gone, Mollie. The church's money is gone. Someone took it from my office."

Mollie stared into his drawn face for only a second before her role as Santa's helper slid away, and her job as Sheriff took over. She looked around, spotted a friend nearby, and beckoned her over. After she'd arranged for the friend to take over with the kids, Mollie led Pastor Wilson into a hallway leading to the kitchen.

The Pastor leaned back against the wall and rubbed his face with both hands. He was a tall, thin handsome man with thick brown hair in his mid-forties like Mollie, and the most caring and dedicated man she had ever known.

"Are you sure, Jimmy? Could the money have just been misplaced?"

"No. I keep the money in a bank pouch in a locked drawer of my desk. The drawer's been jimmied open, and the pouch is gone."

"Was the office door locked?"

"Yes. I always keep the door locked." He tried a feeble smile. "Deliver them from temptation, you know?"

Mollie nodded. "Sometimes that's not

enough. How much money was taken?"

"All the offerings from this week's services, plus the contributions that came in the mail. Altogether, over sixty-two hundred dollars, more than half of it in cash, the rest in checks."

"Well, whoever took it will have a tough time cashing the checks, but that's still a lot of cash."

"It's an awful lot to us, Mollie. The church exists from one week's offering to the next. Without that money, we won't be able to meet our bills this month."

Mollie placed a hand on his shoulder. "We'll do everything we can to get it back. Can we go to your office?"

"Sure. We can take the back stairs."

Mollie followed the Pastor through the kitchen where two women and a man were so busy filling plates with turkey and all the trimmings they didn't even look up. They took a flight of stairs at the back of the kitchen to the second floor. Mollie hated robberies, but this was worse than any other. Someone had robbed a church. Someone had taken money needed to keep the church open and enable it to continue doing so much good for the community. On Christmas Eve yet.

At the top of the stairs, Pastor Wilson pulled a key from his pocket and unlocked a door. Mollie followed him inside the small room filled with simple furnishings. The Pastor's desk sat in front of bookshelves along the back wall. A sofa and two wingbacked chairs lined another wall, with a small wooden table against the opposite wall crowded with a computer, a printer and scattered sheets of paper.

Mollie followed him behind the desk and saw the drawer that had been forced open. The top edge of the drawer just above the lock was splintered and scratched as if someone had gone at it with a sharp, hard object.

"That's where I always keep the money pouch," he said.

"Okay, we know how whoever did it got the drawer open, but how did they get in the office if the door was locked? Is there another way into this room?"

He pointed to his left. "Only that window there, and it's always locked, too. Besides, we're two floors up. No one could get in that way."

Mollie stepped over to the window and saw no signs of anyone forcing it open. "Jimmy, with tomorrow being Christmas day, I can't get anyone in here to dust for fingerprints or look for any other forensic evidence until day after tomorrow. Please don't touch anything you don't have to until then."

"Whatever you say, Mollie." The Pastor crossed the room and slumped on the sofa. "I still can't believe it happened."

"I know how upset you must be, but I have to ask you some more questions, okay?"

"Sure."

"To start with, who had keys to your office?"

The Pastor looked upward and threw a huge sigh. Mollie wasn't sure if he was aiming his dismay at the ceiling or somewhere much higher.

"Besides mine, there are only two. My wife keeps one at home in case of emergencies, and our cleaning lady has one."

"Are they here tonight?"

"My wife isn't. One of our boys is sick, and she stayed home with him."

"Will you call her right now? Ask her to double check and make sure the key is there."

While the Pastor made the call on his cell phone, Mollie examined the desk. None of the other drawers had been touched. The robber knew exactly what he was after and exactly where it was.

Pastor Wilson closed his cell phone. "Trudy said the key is there."

"Good. Now tell me about the cleaning woman who has the other key."

"I'm sure you know her. Consuela Martinez. She's working in the kitchen tonight."

Mollie knew her and was surprised. Consuela's husband owned a large construction company he built from scratch. They lived in a showplace home and each of them drove a new Hummer. "Consuela works as a cleaning woman?"

"Not for money. She volunteers and won't take a cent for it. She brings her kids with her and makes them work, too. She says they need to learn a work ethic like their dad. Five hundred dollars of the money was from her and her husband. A cash donation."

"Good for her," Mollie said. She would still talk to Consuela. You never know. Maybe the generous lady's husband's business wasn't doing well, and she wanted her five hundred back and more.

"When did you last see the pouch?"

The Pastor leaned back against the sofa and rubbed his face with his hands again. "I came up here about a quarter past seven to take out money to pay for another delivery of food from McAllister's Grocery store. The McAllister's have been great to us. They only charged us half for everything. I was only in here a few minutes. After I took out what I needed, I locked up the pouch, locked the door, and went back downstairs."

"And when did you discover the money was missing?"

"About eight o'clock. I had to come up again to get more paper cups from our supply closet. It's right over there." He nodded to his right to a door beside the bookshelves behind his desk. That's when I saw the drawer was open. I came straight down to tell you about it."

Mollie glanced over at the supply closet door. The timing left a forty-five-minute window of opportunity for someone to – somehow – get into the locked office and take the money pouch.

Mollie settled into a chair facing the Pastor. "All right," she said, "let's talk about anyone else who knew where you kept the money. Was anyone in here who might have seen you put the pouch in your drawer?"

"No, no one. Wait a minute. Chuck Handly stopped in while I was counting out the money I needed, but he only stayed a minute or two. He's also working in the kitchen tonight, and he said a water pipe under the sink had a small leak. He said he could do a temporary repair and fix it right later on this week. He took the toolbox we keep in the supply closet and left."

"And after he left, you locked up and went downstairs?"

"Yes."

"Are you certain you locked the door when you left?"

"Absolutely certain."

Mollie reached over and patted his hand. "Jimmy, I'm going to do everything I can to get your money back."

"I know you will, Mollie." He took her hand in both of his and gave her a sorrowful smile. "Even if you don't, we'll find a way to keep going. Sometimes, He works in mysterious ways, but things always work out."

"I'm sure they will. Now, I'm going back downstairs. You coming?"

He pushed himself up from the sofa. "Might as well. Nothing I can do up here."

Mollie led the way out of the office and waited while he locked the door behind them. She heard a soft metallic "click" when he turned the key and the deadbolt slid into place. She tried the door and found it solidly locked.

As she followed the Pastor down the stairs, Mollie kept thinking about those mysterious ways he'd mentioned. What mystery did He have in mind when He stranded her husband in Chicago? Another wave of loneliness washed over her. She and Lilburn had their own tradition for celebrating Christmas Eve. It involved moderate portions of strawberry Margaritas and generous portions of nakedness. With luck, the weather would clear, and he'd make it home the next day. Or the day after that. Or. . .

Once they were down in the kitchen, Pastor Wilson continued on out into the Community Hall. Mollie stayed behind. Consuela Martinez was busy stirring a huge pot of mashed potatoes on the stove. Mollie heard the short, round woman with large brown eyes humming "Jingle Bells" as she worked.

"Mmmmm," Mollie said. "Looks delicious."

Consuela stopped stirring and smiled. "Hi, Mollie. Do you want some? I'll fix you a plate."

"No thanks. I ate earlier. The dinner was

terrific."

"Glad you liked it. I hope you saved room for apple pie and ice cream."

Mollie rubbed her belly and groaned. "I don't know where I'd put it. I'm stuffed."

"Well, there's plenty if you change your mind."

"Thanks, Consuela. Is your husband here?"

"He sure is. That big bear of mine is out there with the kids and working on his second plate. If he eats any more, I'm going to have to roll him home."

Mollie chuckled. "I know what you mean. Sometimes I feel the same way about my husband on holidays. How's his business doing, by the way?"

"Wonderful. He had the best year ever, and he has a big new contract starting after the first of the year. His problem now is hiring enough people to get the work done. Good, dependable workers are hard to find."

Just then, Chuck Handly, a large man with an unruly mop of blond hair, entered the kitchen pushing a cart loaded with dirty plates and silverware. "We're gonna need another load, Consuela. More people just came in. Hi, Mollie. Get enough to eat?"

"Too much, Chuck. How've you been? I haven't seen you for awhile."

"I've been taking jobs out of town, what with the plant cutbacks and all."

"You were laid off?"

"Yeah, and it looks like it'll be a while before they call us back. I been picking up a little work here and there to keep going." He pushed the cart past Mollie and started unloading the dirty dishes into the sink.

Mollie followed him. "Pastor Wilson told me you fixed a leaky pipe tonight. You're handy to have around."

He shrugged. "I do what I can for the church."

Mollie leaned over and looked under the sink. A large open toolbox sat on the floor. In its top liftout drawer were an assortment of screwdrivers, wrenches and pliers and the remains of a roll of duct tape. She saw a copper pipe leading from the wall to the sink basin with a generous wrapping of the tape around it.

"So that's how you stopped the leak," she said.

"Yup. I don't know how we got along before duct tape was invented. I'll replace the pipe in a few days, but till then, it's good as gold. You can stop anything with duct tape."

Mollie laughed. "That's what my Lilburn always says." She saw a small piece of the tape lying on the floor and, out of habit, picked it up. She looked around for a trash can and spotted one by the stove. When she tried to drop the tape in the can, it stuck to her fingers. She pulled it free with her other hand and let it fall. She felt her finger where the tape had stuck. It was sticky. Some of the adhesive had stayed on. She reached for a paper towel from a roll hanging on the wall and wiped at it. No good. The adhesive stayed put.

"Here," Chuck said. He opened a cabinet over the sink and pulled out a bar of soap. "This has a little grit in it. It'll take that right off."

When he closed the cabinet, Mollie heard a tiny metallic "click" similar to the one she'd heard upstairs. The handle on the cabinet door moved a sliding bolt like the dead bolt lock on Pastor Wilson's office door.

Chuck moved over to give Mollie room to wash her hands. As she did, she kept thinking about the sliding bolts, the duct tape, and what Chuck had said.

"You can stop anything with duct tape."

By the time she'd finished washing and drying her hands, Chuck was on his way to the Community Hall with another cartload of dinners. Mollie followed him out and found the Pastor talking to Consuela's husband. She went over to him and asked him to follow her back upstairs to his office. On their way through the kitchen, she picked up the roll of duct tape and a utility knife from the toolbox under the sink. Once upstairs, she asked the Pastor to unlock the door again.

With the door open, Mollie rubbed her finger around the opening where the dead bolt slid back inside the door. When she raised her finger, she felt the same adhesive she'd felt down in the kitchen.

The Pastor watched silently, but finally asked, "Uh, Mollie, what are you doing?"

"Jimmy, Chuck Handly is the one who robbed your office and I know how. Let me show you." She cut a short piece from the roll of duct tape and pressed it over the hole the bolt slid out of. Then she asked the Pastor to close and lock the door.

Once he'd done as she asked, Mollie pushed on the door and it opened.

The Pastor moved closer and examined where the tape prevented the bolt from sliding into the hole in the door jamb as it normally would.

He shook his head. "If I hadn't seen it, I wouldn't have believed it. That's amazing, Mollie, but how in the world did he lock the door again? When I came back up, it was definitely locked."

Mollie frowned. "I'm still working on that." After a few moments, she said, "I've got it!"

She cut another piece of tape, longer this time. She removed the first piece of tape and applied the second one. This time, she left the long end of the tape sticking out and closed the door. Then she took hold of the piece of tape sticking out and pulled on it. The tape came all the way out, freeing the bolt, and she heard the "click" as it slid into place. She pushed on the door to make sure it was solidly locked. It was.

"Jimmy, when Chuck came up to get the toolbox, he saw you putting the money away. When he left your office, he cut a piece of tape and stuck it over the bolt hole the same way I did. He waited till you came downstairs and sneaked back up here. You thought you'd locked the door, but you really hadn't because of the tape. He probably used a screwdriver from the toolbox to bust into the drawer. Then he taped the door like I just did on his way out, pulled out the tape, and the door locked again."

The Pastor wagged his head. "That poor, poor man. I knew he was having a rough time after he was laid off, but I never dreamed he'd do something like this. This is so hard to believe."

"Maybe in your business it is, Jimmy. Not in mine. Let's go down to the kitchen.

I have another hunch."

In the kitchen, Mollie went directly to the toolbox and lifted out the top drawer. In the bottom part of the box she saw a cluttering of more wrenches, screwdrivers, and boxes of nails and screws. She rooted down beneath all that and brought out the missing money pouch.

She handed it to the Pastor. "He probably figured on taking it out to his car as soon as he had a chance."

The Pastor took a deep breath and let it out slowly. "I still find it hard to believe Chuck would do something like this."

"Well, Jimmy, as much as I hate doing it, while you're trying to figure it out, I have to find him and arrest him."

She started to walk away, but he touched her arm. "Mollie, is that really necessary?"

"Jimmy, I don't like it any better than you do, but he broke the law."

"I know, but he's had a really rough time since he lost his job. Desperate times make people do things they wouldn't ordinarily do. Did you know his wife is sick and they have four children?"

"No, I didn't know that, but I still have to take him in and charge him."

"Please, Mollie, let me talk to him. I've known him for a lot of years, and I know he'll repent and never do anything like this again. He's a good man, and after all, the church has its money back. No real harm has been done."

"Jimmy, I know what you're saying, but I have to. . ."

The Pastor placed his hands on her shoulders. "Mollie, can you really take him away from his family on this night? It's Christmas Eve, a time when people should be with their loved ones."

Mollie rubbed the back of her neck, something she always did when she was perplexed, and paced back and forth. Finally, she said, "All right, Jimmy, here's what I can do. I'll release him in your custody, but you have to bring him to my office first thing

Monday morning. We'll talk to Judge Harrison about getting him a suspended sentence and probation."

"Do you think Judge Harrison will agree?"

"I think he will. He's a fair and compassionate man." Mollie winked. "Besides, he'd better agree if he wants my Lilburn to come over and fix his computer next time he crashes it."

"If a computer fix is what it takes, then so be it. As I said before, He often works in mysterious ways. And, Mollie, a kindness like you're doing doesn't go unnoticed. You'll see. Somehow, what you're doing for Chuck and his family will come back to you, even if it's in . . ."

She waved it off and grinned. "I know, Jimmy, I know. In mysterious ways."

He laughed. "I'll go talk to Chuck now. Why don't you have some of that wonderful apple pie and ice cream Consuela made?"

"Maybe I will. And, by the way, if Chuck is serious about finding a job, tell him to talk to Consuela's husband. He's looking for a few good men."

Twenty minutes later, Mollie sat at a table by herself in the Community Hall eating apple pie. A small piece, and she'd passed on the ice cream. Santa had packed up and gone back to the North Pole, and she had nothing else to do. The sounds of families enjoying

Christmas Eve surrounded her, but she still couldn't get in the mood.

"It's Christmas Eve," Pastor Jimmy had said, *"a time when people should be with their loved ones."*

Yeah, right, Mollie thought. *Everyone but me.*

When her cell phone rang, she answered reluctantly. She expected it to be someone from the station house with a question or a problem.

Instead, a familiar voice said, "Hey, hon, guess what."

"Lilburn! What?"

"The weather broke and some flights were able to get out. I hopped on one at the very last second."

"Where are you?"

"I just landed and I'm waiting for my luggage. I'll be home in fifteen minutes. Are you still at the church? How soon can you get away?"

When she didn't respond for several moments, he said, "Mollie, you still there?"

"I'm still here."

"I thought I lost you for a minute."

"Oh, I was just thinking about mysterious ways."

"Uh...what do you mean?"

"Never mind. I'll tell you when I see you. You go on home and mix up a pitcher of Christmas cheer, and I'll be there before you can fill the glasses."

"Great! Merry Christmas Eve, Mollie."
"Just wait till I get home. I'm going to show you what merry is all about."

Copyright ©2007 Earl Staggs

The Lesson of the Season
Thomas H. Cook

It was the final minutes of the final day before Christmas, and Veronica Cross wanted only to pass these last moments sitting silently behind the register, her attention fixed on the book that rested in her lap. She had worked at the Mysterious Bookshop for almost ten years, but only on Saturdays, when the owner was at his house in Connecticut, and the store's full-time employees were scattered about various apartments throughout the city. Her job was simply to buzz customers into the store, answer whatever questions they asked, take their money, bag their purchases, then buzz them back out onto 56th street. Almost no intellectual energy was required on Veronica's part, and the small financial supplement her salary added to her "real job" as a freelance copy editor made it possible for her to buy books from other stores, along with an occasional dinner out, or perhaps a discount ticket to a Broadway show.

The dinner and show might be enjoyed alone or with one of her friends, someone like herself, who read good books and could articulately discuss them. As for romance, she'd more or less given up on that. Most men were little boys, needy and selfish, and none had ever struck her as worth the effort it took to dress up and preen and put on a happy face when she well knew that after the first few minutes she'd want only to hail a cab, return home, crawl into bed and open a book.

As for dress, she opted for modest elegance, long solid-colored skirts and dark-hued blouses for the most part, though black jeans with an accompanying black turtleneck sweater were not beyond her. Physically, she was tall, lithesome, and incontestably attractive, but for all that she preferred to blend into whatever woodwork surrounded her. That other people chased distant stars, felt imperial urges, sought fame, or at least notoriety, all of that was a mystery to Veronica because she wished only to be left alone with her books.

She glanced at the clock at the rear of the room, then at her watch to verify the clock's correctness. Both sentenced her to fifteen more minutes of minding the store, and given the heavy snow that had begun to fall outside, she thought it quite likely that she might be able to pass those final moments lost in her book, the store silent all around her, with nothing but the soft tick, tick of the clock to remind her that she was part of an all too human world.

Then it happened.

Someone buzzed.

Veronica glanced toward the door, recognized the mild, faintly hang-dog face she saw behind the glass, then pressed the buzzer and let him in.

His name was Harry Bentham, and he came to the store every Saturday, though usually not during the final minutes of the day, and never during the final minutes of the final day before Christmas when a heavy snow was falling outside.

"Hi," Harry said quietly as he stepped into the shop.

"Hi," Veronica replied in a voice that was not without welcome, but which did nothing to encourage a more extended greeting.

Harry slapped the melting flakes of snow that had accumulated on the shoulders of his worn gray overcoat and stepped nearer to one of the shelves.

Veronica returned to her book, knowing exactly what she would see should she glance up again: Harry facing a shelf of paperback novels, his wiry gray hair blinking dully in the overhanging light, his rounded shoulders slumped, his posture no less slumped, so that he seemed perpetually to be collapsing, or if not that, then held up by invisible strings that were themselves stretched and frayed and in imminent danger of snapping.

But saddest of all, Veronica thought, was that Harry never bought a good book, and thus had yet to experience the actual thrill of literature, the way a fine passage could lift you high above the teeming world, give you focus and a sense of proportion, allow a small life to expand.

In the years of Saturdays Veronica had spent behind the register, she'd come to divide humanity into those who read good books and those who read bad ones. As for Harry, he topped the list of readers who seemed to have no sense of what a book was for, that it could pull you deeper into life, direct your concentration toward things that really mattered, give voice to longing, prepare you for death. At no time during the ten years of her stewardship had Harry ever bought a hardback book. He had rarely even risen to the level of literature that had at least been briefly housed between hard covers. No, Harry was not only a reader of bad books, he was a reader of paperback originals, a reader of works so entirely without merit, so utterly devoid of any enduring quality of style or story or idea, that even the work's publisher had opted to present it in a form doomed to vanish at the first approach of mold.

"Uh..." Harry said tentatively. "Veronica?"

Veronica looked up from her book.

"You don't have the new Bruno Klem, do you?" Bruno Klem was the author of a decidedly lowbrow series of paperback originals known to its few aficionados as "The Crime Beat Chronicles." From the garish covers, the novels appeared to take place in a neon lit city of strip clubs and after hours bars in which he-man detective Franklin Lord battled the dastardly minions of Oslo Sinestre, the series' arch villain.

"It hasn't come in yet," Veronica said. She offered a quick smile, then returned her attention to *The Measure of Man,* a book which was, according to the jacket copy, "a beautifully written and philosophically astute meditation on the moral complexity of human life as seen through the eyes of a defrocked Venezuelan priest."

She turned the page. "We live in the echo of our pain," she read silently.

She glanced up from the book and watched Harry's back, the way his right hand lifted tentatively toward a particular book, then drew away and sank again into the pocket of his frayed coat. He was no doubt preparing to make a selection, and she found herself hoping that something would seize him suddenly, direct his attention to the neighboring shelf where he might find a work of actual merit, one that would enlarge his appreciation of what a book can do, how it can draw you down to previously unplumbed depths of understanding.

But Harry remained in place, and so Veronica returned her attention to the book.

We live in the echo of our pain.

She pondered the phrase and for some reason, impossible to fathom, found herself seated near her father's hospital bed, the old man stretched out on his back, tubes running here and there, an oxygen mask over his mouth and nose, so that he looked like an

41

astronaut carefully strapped in for the outward voyage.

He had died eight years before, when Veronica had been twenty-one years old, living in her Park Slope apartment—Manhattan being far too expensive—and eking out the same modest living in the same poorly paid trade she still practiced. She'd sat with him each night during the final days of his life, done what she thought required of an only child, the daughter of a divorced father who'd outlived not only her mother, but the two wives he'd later married and divorced, so that by the time of his final illness, there'd been no one who felt the slightest obligation toward him, save Veronica. He had been a wealthy real estate agent until suddenly, at the first onset of middle age, he'd gone completely nuts, sold the agency, and begun spending money hand over fist or losing vast quantities of it in cruelly expensive divorce settlements.

Year by year his fortune had dwindled, until the last of it had vanished by the time Veronica had graduated from high school, selected an Ivy League college, applied, been accepted, then learned to her shock and dismay that her father had even squandered the money he had previously set aside for her education, spending every penny of it on high-roller gambling trips to Las Vegas, extravagant parties at the Pierre, wining and dining an army of fortune-seeking bimbos, and finally on a yacht he'd anchored briefly off Fire Island, then sold at a huge loss to an oil man from Houston. The yacht had been the old man's last costly asset, and he'd used the proceeds of its sale on such stylish perishables as watches and hand-tailored suits, all of which he had later palmed off to various Second Avenue consignment shops, after which, with truly nothing left, he had sunk into absolute penury.

As a result, Veronica had been forced to waitress during the day and at night attend classes at Hunter College, from which she had finally graduated, but with a diploma that could not compete with the Ivy League educated and equally striking coeds who thronged about the great publishing houses of New York. Thus, she had been relegated to the decidedly unglamorous world of freelance editors, living from manuscript to manuscript, and thus from hand to mouth, a condition to which she had adapted quite well. In recent years, she had even concluded that hers was a superior position since she didn't have to kiss anyone's ass and could, with few exceptions, select the titles she wished to edit and avoid the utter trash that salaried employees could not.

We live in the echo of our pain.

She turned the phrase over in her mind, and wondered why it had returned her to her father's bedside during his bleak final days, the smelly hospital ward in which she'd sat night after night, and which she had only left after he'd released his last breath. It was miraculous, really, the way a few words could summon you back to past experiences, illuminate the shadowy corridors of that backward journey, allow it to resonate within you. Such was the true value of literature, she decided, that it gave life a resounding echo.

"You don't read Bruno Klem?"

Veronica glanced up to see Harry Bentham staring at her, his face barely visible behind the huge black plastic frames of his glasses.

"No, I don't."

Harry nodded slowly and turned back to the shelves, moving his face closer to the individual paperback spines, intently focused on each one, as far as Veronica could tell, as if he were searching for the answer to life among the volumes he found there.

But what answer could he possibly expect to find among the paperback originals, Veronica wondered. Where in any of those inferior volumes could pain's echo rise from the page and in that rising address the great mystery of how we came to be the one we are, how we should proceed, what we should seek in the brevity of our days, and what forgo? In a room filled with mysteries, this seemed the deepest of them all, one Veronica now determined to have answered at least as far as Harry Bentham could answer it.

She closed *The Measure of Man* and sat back, pressing her spine against the wall behind her. "I have a question," she said.

Harry turned, clearly surprised that she had addressed him.

"Why do you read Bruno Klem?"

Harry's thick, eerily purplish lips parted mutely.

"Every Saturday you come in here and buy five or six books," Veronica added. "Always Bruno Klem, or something like it. So, my question is, what do you get out of it? I'd really like to know."

Harry blinked slowly, removed his glasses, wiped them with a handkerchief drawn from his back pocket, and returned them to his face. "'They're like a scotch to me," he said.

"A scotch?"

"You know, like when you come home at the end of a bad day, and maybe your wife is waiting for you, and she gives you a scotch."

Veronica knew that Harry Bentham had never been married, that no one waited for him with a drink in hand at the end of the day, but that was not the point.

"A book is a scotch?" she asked. "What does that mean?" She shook her head in exasperation. "Let me try a different direction. When did you start reading?"

"During the war," Harry said.

Judging by Harry's age, Veronica guessed that he meant the Vietnam War, but the precise military conflict to which he had referred was in no sense the issue. "When you were young then?" she asked.

"During the war," Harry repeated.

"Because you were bored?"

"No."

"Why then?"

Harry shrugged silently. He seemed reluctant to go on.

Veronica, however, was in no mood to take silence for an answer. "Why then?" she repeated.

"We came in from a patrol" Harry answered. "Went to our tents. There was a book on one of the cots. "

"What kind of book?"

"A little paperback," Harry said. He nodded toward the wall of paperback originals that rose behind him. "Bruno Klem." He shrugged again, his shoulders rising and falling ponderously. "The sergeant saw me moping around. He tossed me the book. 'Here,' he said, 'it'll take your mind off it.'"

"Off what?" Veronica asked.

"The patrol," Harry answered. "It was a bad patrol."

"Bad in what way?"

Harry drew in a long breath, one that trembled slightly. "We were all around this old man. Asking him questions. He was shaking his head no, he didn't know anything. We kept yelling and he kept shaking his head, you know?"

Veronica imagined the scene, Harry in

his raw youth, small and bespectacled, his round shoulders slumped beneath the weight of whatever soldiers carry, canteens and ammo belts and some kind of rifle. He'd probably been the company geek, slow and ineffectual, a burden to the others. More than anything she imagined him naive and innocent, a kid who'd stumbled into the army the way he might have stumbled into a job at the nearest shoe store and kept it for fifty years.

"It was really hot, and we'd lost some guys," Harry continued. "And the old man just kept shaking his head and saying he didn't know where the others were, the VC, I mean, the ones who'd killed, you know, some of us."

Now she saw him in a tight circle of other soldiers, all of them wet with sweat, covered in jungle debris, Harry the smallest, the least involved in the interrogation of the old man, wanting only to get away, find a little shade, take a listless snooze.

"Anyway, I started getting mad, you know?"

She could not imagine Harry Bentham mad any more than she could imagine him smart or passionate or good in bed. He was part of the great gray herd, a reader of trash, solitary, a flat-liner, J. Alfred Prufrock anesthetized upon a table.

"Mad?" she asked. "You?"

He seemed hardly to hear her, his eyes now distant, but oddly charged, a strange, unsettling gleam replacing his usual dull stare.

"Something takes you," he said quietly. "It comes and it takes you."

She could feel a wave of heat coming from him, fierce and violent, as if from a raging furnace.

"Takes you," he repeated, almost to himself. "And you're gone.

He jerked his right hand from the pocket of his overcoat and formed it into a fleshy pistol, the index finger as its barrel.

"And so I yelled at him, and he kept saying no, and it was so hot, and I started yelling louder because we'd lost all these guys and so..." The index finger curled into a trigger finger and Harry's hand jerked. "So... I" He stopped, thought a moment, then added. "The other guys said it could happen to anybody. War and all. But it was murder. You can't deny it. It was murder, pure and simple."

He sank his hand deep into the pocket of his overcoat, and his voice lowered and its pace slowed to a melancholy crawl. "You think you're one thing, then suddenly, you're something else." His closed his eyes slowly, then opened them again. "Anyway, when I got back to camp, the Sergeant tossed me this book and said it would take my mind off of it." A small, mournful smile played on his lips, and his eyes glistened. "We all have things we want to forget, don't we?"

Suddenly, Veronica was with her father again, sitting in a chair, staring at him coldly, listening as his breath swept raggedly in and out until suddenly his eyes opened, and in a struggling tone, he called her name.

"Don't we?" Harry asked.

She saw herself rise and walk to the side of his bed, his eyes barely open, his lips moving frantically, repeating her name, *Veronica, Veronica.* She saw in his eyes a strangely desperate pleading, and felt that he was perhaps asking her forgiveness for the hardship to which his reckless self-indulgence had sentenced her. She started to answer him, soothe him, tell him that she loved him, that all was forgiven. But suddenly she considered the wasted fortune, the gray rooms of night school, her long days at a greasy diner, the cramped Brooklyn apartment, and a jolt of consuming anger shot through her, hot and jangling as a vicious electrical charge.

"Things we did, that ... you know..."

Now she was staring at the old man sullenly, coldly watching as his eyes closed and his lips parted breathlessly, her hand rising all the while, rising as if drawn into the air by a vast malignant power, furious, demented by rage, rising and rising, until it finally stopped, held an instant, then swept down in blistering fury, and in the echoing horror of the moment, she realized that she had slapped her dead father's face.

"... things... we can't take back."

She drew in a shaky breath and all but shuddered in that remembered rage, all the fuming anger of her lost ambitions, her father's mad indifference, the blighted life that had been his, and which to some degree she had inherited, all of it in full, resounding echo, moving in seething waves over and within and through her.

"Yes," she said. "We do."

Harry nodded. "Anyway, the book worked," he said. "I been reading them ever since."

She thought of Harry now, the echoing violence in which he lived, how it must endlessly swell and eddy in dark and bloody currents, Bruno Klem the wall he raised against them, and behind which he labored to secure a simple, decent life. What had he been before that distant murder, she wondered. What life had he imagined for himself? Had he even remotely guessed that in that single pistol blast he would equally destroy a future wife and children, a life lived in something other than the moral bafflement that now held his heart in thrall, and from which he sought brief escape in the preposterous antics of paperback heroes who shot it out with unreal villains in worlds where the moral lines were never blurred.

She rose, walked over to the shelf behind Harry and drew out the first paperback installment of a new action series. Then she turned and handed him the book, softly, affectionately, as she thought a loving wife might hand him a scotch at the end of a long, bad day. "Try this," she said. "It's by a new author. There'll be lots of books in the series."

Harry took the book. "Thanks," he said, then paid her and left the store, his shoulders hunched against the outer chill, the falling snow

Veronica returned to her place, retrieved *The Measure of Man* from where she'd placed it on top of the register, and opened it.

We live in the echo of our pain.

The line was still moving through her mind a few minutes later when she placed the book in her bag, turned out the lights, locked the door, and thus secured the merely literary mysteries behind an iron gait.

On the long subway ride to her small, book-stuffed studio in Park Slope, she sat silently, with her hands in her lap. Normally, she would have read her book during the ride home, kept her eyes fixed on the words, turned the pages without ever looking up. But now she took time to consider the other people on the train, wondering what dark, unspoken things might have befallen them, what sorrows they had suffered, witnessed, caused, the varied ways they'd managed to endure the life that followed. In all of that, we were the same, she decided, bent on finding comfort in whatever way we can.

Once she'd peered briefly at each face opposite her, she lifted her eyes to the lighted advertising panel that shone above them. It showed a Christmas tree. On a busy corner, a man in uniform holding a red bucket, people dropping change into charity's deep well. She drew her gaze from the photograph, thought of Harry, then of herself, then of the others on the train, in the city, on the planet.

It was the lesson of the season, she supposed, that all of them... are you.

Copyright ©2003 Thomas H. Cook

Santa and the Poor Box
Gail Farrelly

Two weeks before Christmas, and I'm listening to holiday music from the fifties as I sit paying bills at my computer in the corner of the living room. When "Jingle Bell Rock" comes on, I have to pause for a moment and just enjoy it. That was what I was listening to on this same day a year ago when my 14-year-old daughter asked her forty-something widowed mom for a very special Christmas gift—helping to mount a defense in a case that seemed indefensible.

I look at the garland of tinsel and holly carelessly draped over my computer (lacking a decorator's eye, I still try to do some decorating, really I do!) and recall how it shook last year when my daughter Lily returned from her friend's house and came storming in, slamming our heavy front door behind her. No hello or how are you. She simply took off her white ski jacket, threw it on a chair, and then draped her slim body on the navy blue velour couch next to the computer.

"It's an outrage!" was her greeting. "They have Santa Claus in jail, and I'm sure he didn't do anything."

I had read the story in the local paper about a Santa Claus working a Christmas promotion at the local A&P. He'd been arrested on the charge of burglarizing the neighborhood church a few nights ago. "Oh, you mean the old guy who broke into the poor box at church?" I said. This was big news in a small, quiet town like ours in the suburbs of New York City.

Lily tugged at her ponytail in frustration. "They say he broke into the poor box, but I don't believe it, not for a minute. No way."

"Maybe he was desperate, honey. Sometimes people are, you know."

Lily sighed. "Desperate, that's how I feel, Mom. He's innocent. Someone has to help him. His name is Kris Taylor, and he's a Vietnam Vet, was shot twice there. He must be in his sixties. He's been homeless a lot, jobless too. Now he lives in a rooming house in the Bronx. And he said the A&P might even keep him on after Christmas. He's been such a hit as Santa, they may hire him to play other characters for different holidays. But now this. What rotten luck for him."

"How did you find out all this stuff?" I asked, amazed and appalled that she knew so much about this total stranger, possibly a thief.

"He told me," she said, a slight tone of belligerence in her voice. "I talked to him last week when I was working outside the A&P, selling chances for the raffle for our teen group. He's a good guy, Mom. I'm sure of it."

I hated to shatter her innocence, but I

said, "Well according to the paper, they have a witness. And forensic evidence too."

"I don't care what they have. He didn't do it. Someone claimed the thief was a Santa Claus. So what? Anyone can dress up as Santa Claus. Remember when I was a kid and you took me to Macy's to see Santa? You said he was the real thing. That all the others around town dressed as Santa were just his helpers." She paused, a little smile on her face. Her voice was louder when she continued. "What a crock!" Another pause. "But this guy *is* the real thing. A really good person, I mean. I could tell."

I sighed and said, "But sometimes good people do bad things, honey."

"And good people could do good things. Like you. You're smart. You know a lot of cops, big shots, and a bunch of other people. You could look into the case, see what's going on, maybe get him the help he needs. I'm sure he's not guilty."

I shrugged. "I'm really busy at work these days. I'm sure he has a public defender."

"A public defender may not be enough." She got up from the couch and looked me straight in the eye. She looked like she was going to cry. "This morning you asked me what I wanted for Christmas. This is it. I want you to see what's going on and help people see who Kris Taylor really is. Then they'll let him out of jail." She let this sink in before continuing. "Yep, that's my Christmas present. Get Santa Claus out of jail." Not sure of how to reply, I kept my mouth shut. As she turned to leave the room, she fired a parting shot. "Daddy would do it if he were still here."

The kid made a helluva closing argument.

***

The morning after that ultimatum I was sitting in a room at the county jail, glad that it was a Saturday and I didn't have to miss work. Waiting to meet Kris Taylor, I thought about how the movie *Miracle on 34th Street* made helping Santa Claus seem charming and easy. In real life, it was probably neither. But still, as the widow of a New York City police detective killed on 9/11, I would have many doors open to me that would be closed to some others. Following the dictum of the late Tug McGraw, I told myself, "Ya gotta believe."

I nervously ran my fingers through my short brown hair, wishing that I was at the beauty parlor getting my gray roots covered. Oh heck, I wished I was anyplace else but here. I focused on what I had read in the newspaper that morning as well as what I had been able to squeeze out of a 'source' at the D.A.'s office in an early morning phone call. Apparently the assistant D.A. in charge of the case was sure she had the goods. They had a witness who claimed she could identify him as the thief. In addition, Kris's fingerprints were on the raided poor box. Most damning of all, they found several hundred dollars in his possession when he was picked up. And this was a man who appeared to live from paycheck to paycheck. Three strikes and he was out.

I tried not to stare when a female jail attendant opened the door and escorted Taylor into the room. She told him to take the chair across the table from me and said she'd be right outside the door. "You have only a few minutes," she said, glancing at her watch, adding "It's almost lunch time."

He looked like a character right out of central casting. Call and say you needed someone to play Santa Claus and this guy would definitely fit the bill. The perfect Santa, even though he was garbed in a prison jumpsuit of dull gray, rather than the traditional red-and-white suit with the black belt. I found myself tongue-tied at first, but I did get my act together, shook his hand and said, "I'm Roberta McHugh. My daughter Lily met you last week with her teen group outside the A&P. She asked me to come here, see if I could help."

He sat down and said, "Call me Kris. Thanks for coming. Yeah, I remember Lily. The one who wants to be an attorney." I was taken aback. This guy knew something about my daughter that I didn't. I was grateful for the heads up and decided then and there to put more money in her education fund. Law school was expensive.

It was hard to focus, as I took in the red cheeks, the round stomach, even the beard. That beautiful, perfect, fluffy white beard. Maybe the staring gave me away or perhaps he could read my mind or something, because suddenly he gave his beard a tug, grinned, and said, "Yep, it's real, there's nothing phony about me." He shrugged but smiled as he did so. Amazing that he seemed quite calm.

Time for me to get down to business. "The paper says they have a witness."

He nodded agreement. "Apparently an old lady praying in the back of church says she saw Santa Claus steal from the poor box and swore it was the A&P Santa." He sighed. "Why wasn't she saying her prayers at home in the middle of the night? The police say the robbery happened at about 2 a.m. I was asleep in my rooming house in the Bronx but have no witnesses. It's not the kind of place where you mind the other guy's business."

"Got it. But your fingerprints were found on the poor box, right?"

"Yeah, but apparently there were a number of prints. At least that's what I heard through the grapevine. Also heard that the box had been polished earlier in the day. If it hadn't been, I'm sure there would have been many more prints. I was in the church that day and put some change *into* the poor box, so sure my fingerprints were there. So what? Believe me, I didn't do anything wrong."

"Okay. Now, about the money they

found on you. You have to admit that over $300 in cash was an awful lot to be carrying around. And it *is* kind of suspicious that you wouldn't reveal where you had gotten it."

For the first time, he looked positively furious. "That's my money. That's all I'll say. I've watched Perry Mason and know it's my right to keep my mouth shut. Plain and simple, I'm no thief. I did *not* break into that poor box. Sure I've had some scrapes with the law over the years. Did some panhandling where I wasn't supposed to, stole some food when I was hungry, but steal from a poor box? Fuggedaboutit. And if I was gonna rob a church, I sure wouldn't wear my Santa gear."

Seemed reasonable, but maybe that was because I kept thinking about this guy as Santa Claus. Still, if he hadn't stolen it, what was so secretive about the money he was carrying? I said, "But maybe if you told them where you got the money, this whole matter could be straightened out."

He wasn't impressed with my suggestion. "I'm not going there. It's my business, no one else's."

"Well yeah. But you're the one stuck in jail. You might have to make a choice about your right to privacy or your right to freedom."

He gave a sad smile. "Yeah, I realize that." A pause. "My past isn't lily white, so it's easy to jump to conclusions. That's how they're able to hold me here. And of course they came and arrested me the very next day after the robbery. But still—I know my rights."

"I'll tell you this. If Lily were running things here, she'd release you in a minute. She says you're one of the good guys."

"Tell her thanks from me. Maybe I'm crazy… well, probably I am crazy, but I have this feeling things will turn around and *someone* will help me out."

I squirmed a little, since I figured he was targeting me. I wanted to scream, "Speak up. Spill the beans about the money in your pocket." But instead I said, "I'm willing to see what I can do but won't make any promises. You do have a public defender, don't you?"

"Yeah, an earnest, overworked young man who seems to think my case is hopeless." He gave a wry smile and added, "I think he's one of those guys who doesn't believe in Santa Claus." I was thinking of a reply when the jail attendant arrived back in the room and indicated that our time was up. Good. Interview over. With a swift "Thanks for coming," Kris was gone.

I sat there for a minute planning my strategy. I looked at my watch and then fished my cell phone from my purse. First things first. A fool thinking she could rescue Santa at least should not look like an *old* fool. Two minutes later I had booked an appointment at the beauty parlor for later that day to get my hair colored.

***

"So you think you can do something for him, Mom?" Lily asked that night, in between bites of pizza and salad, a hastily prepared supper. "By the way, your hair looks cool."

"Thanks, honey. I'll do what I can for Kris, but it won't be easy. And I doubt we can expect too much from his public defender."

I then spent a few minutes filling her in about my meeting with the public defender. I had been able to see him in the time between the jail visit and my hair appointment; our meeting confirmed what I had suspected. An exhausted-looking young man, toiling away on a Saturday in a tiny cubicle cluttered with unfiled papers, post-it notes, and all sorts of evidence of an enormous caseload, would probably not have a lot of time or resources to devote to this one particular case. Of course he reminded me that his client had pleaded not guilty, but his eyes told me what his lips didn't. He definitely thought his client was guilty.

Lily listened to my public defender report and then said, "He's a jerk. That's the establishment for you."

"Tell me about it," I said, as I reached over for another slice of pizza. "But not having a formal connection to what you call 'the establishment' could work to our advantage. Knowing all the people around town that we do, maybe we can sniff out some important points."

"Way to go, mom," said my delighted daughter.

I smiled at the compliment but held out my right hand like a traffic cop and said, "Save the congratulations. We'll have to see what develops."

"Okay, so tell me more about what happened today," Lily said.

"Well, I don't really think the eyewitness thing will hold up. The old lady must have seen a Santa Claus…"

"But not necessarily *our* Santa, right?" an excited Lily responded.

"Exactly. The witness has terrible eyesight."

"Of course, Mom. I could have told you that. I talked to Meredith, that girl from the teen club, and she knows who the old lady is. She lives down the street from her. Meredith says the old lady's glasses are really, really thick. And she's a pesty old biddy, always complaining about noise or something or other. Loves attention."

"Hey, you've been busy," I said.

Lily smiled. "I wasn't going to sit by and let you do all the work. But I'm glad we both found out the same thing about that so-called witness."

"Yeah. A good defense attorney could rip her to shreds. Even a not-so-good one could probably do the job."

"Right," Lily responded. "Next up, the fingerprints on the poor box. I read about it in the paper. What gives?"

"Kris explained the prints by saying he had put some put some change *into* the box, but that may be a tough sell to a jury. The detectives are checking a variety of fingerprint databases to see if they can find a match for any of the other prints found on the poor box, but so far no luck." I then went on to explain about the money found on Kris when he was arrested and the suspicions raised when he wouldn't say where he had gotten it.

"But it's not against the law to carry a couple of hundred dollars around, and it's not fair that he should have to make an accounting." Lily sighed. "It's just not fair."

"I know, I know," I said, as Lily reached for the last slice of pizza, cut it in half and give me one of the pieces.

Then she announced, "It's up to us. We have to figure out where Kris got that money. That's where we have to start. It's our only chance. *His* only chance."

She was probably right—unfortunately. I munched on the last of my pizza, thought of Kris, and wondered what he was eating for supper. I also wondered how long he'd be in jail, especially with the likes of the two of us working to free him!

***

But guess what? It wasn't that long. It was just ten days later that Lily made a discovery that set in motion the events that would get him out of jail. Here's what happened.

I had twisted the arms of just about every source I could think of—at my firm and among my acquaintances and friends—to come up with ways of figuring out where Kris had gotten the several hundred dollars found in his pocket. Lily and I were convinced that his freedom depended on it, and we figured that he would never reveal where he had gotten it. Maybe it was an illegal source, maybe not; but in any event, he would never tell.

I was busy at work at that time and could only give a limited amount of time to the 'Kris' project. I helped to direct the search; but it was Lily who did most of the searching. She was relentless, devoting hours every day to work on behalf of her new friend. Finally, on the tenth day of searching, she hit pay dirt. She had read an article on the Web about someone whose life changed when she had received a settlement in a malpractice case. Lily wondered if something like that could have been the source of Kris's money.

Eureka! She was right. The discovery took many hours of work by Lily and the assistance of a skilled and dogged librarian friend of mine. (God bless friends, especially those who happen to be librarians!)

Turns out that a couple of years before his A&P gig, Kris had spent some time in a little town on the Jersey shore and had ended up suing the town, claiming that he had been falsely arrested for loitering. The suit had been settled out of court, and Kris had received a payment of $200,000. Both sides had agreed not to make the details of the settlement public. Yeah, sure, is there anything these days that can be completely kept out of the public eye? Good thing, too, because mention of the lawsuit appeared in an obscure little document (minutes of some committee or other of the town council) Lily unearthed online while she was searching under the direction of my librarian friend. Lily never tires of reminding me, of course, that it was originally *her* idea to check out lawsuit settlements, although she does admit that she never would have been able to find the information without the help of my friend. Hey, no problem. I give credit where it's due. My contribution, in comparison to theirs, was minimal.

    The finding that Kris had a nice nest egg didn't mean he was definitely not guilty, but it did indicate that the couple of hundred dollars in his pocket may not have come from the poor box after all. Chances are this information would have eventually been unearthed by the authorities. Or at some point Kris might have given in and spilled the info about his lawsuit bounty. But without our intervention I don't think this would have happened before Christmas.

    Searching for information to clear Kris was certainly not a high priority of anyone in the justice system, since the police felt they had their man. Things have a way of not being found if you're not looking for them. A stubborn but innocent person could have spent Christmas in jail as a result. And jail just isn't the place for Santa Claus at Christmas.

Anyway, armed with this new information, Lily and I visited Kris in jail to try to convince him to tell the authorities where his money came from. His reaction was mixed. On the one hand, he was annoyed that we had violated his privacy; on the other, he was touched by our concern.

He described the $200,000 settlement as "nobody's business but mine" and "my pension for a lifetime of panhandling and holding down menial, low-paying jobs." He said most people didn't reveal to the public the details of their pension, so why should he? He had a good chunk of cash with him on the day he was picked up, because he was planning to stop off at Sears that night and buy himself a Christmas present, a portable DVD player.

We didn't press our luck and tell him that Lily's research had also unearthed the fact that Kris had donated $50,000 of his settlement to an organization for disabled veterans here in New York. He really was such a study in contrasts.

We finally persuaded Kris to explain the source of his money to the detectives on the case. This didn't get him an immediate release; but it set the wheels in motion so that he could be released on bail. And it breathed new life into the investigation by raising the real possibility that he wasn't guilty.

In our computerized world, we assume that it's relatively easy for needed information to reach the proper people at the proper time. Wrong! This whole episode was a textbook example of how easy it is to take evidence and slot it into categories based on preconceived notions.

Kris put up bail and was released on Christmas Eve. Lily and I picked him up at the jail and invited him to our home for dinner. He looked at us as if we were crazy and said, "Of course not, this is the busiest night of the year for me."

***

Now it's a year later, but I still smile when I think of that response from Kris to our Christmas Eve invitation. And how, after we had dropped him off at his rooming house, Lily turned to me and said she thought maybe he was taking this Santa thing a bit too seriously.

There was a startling turn of events in February of this year. A guy (a druggie high as a kite) in a Mickey Mouse suit was nabbed at a church in Connecticut, attempting to pry open the poor box. His fingerprints matched one of the sets of prints taken on the poor box involved in the crime Kris was accused of. Confronted with the evidence, the guy owned up to the Santa Claus caper in our neighborhood. Whew! Kris Taylor was completely off the hook. A happy ending to last year's Christmas adventure.

Kris has been doing well. For the past year, he's had a full-time job at the A&P as a greeter playing a variety of cartoon characters. A feature story on him recently appeared in the local paper. He's been to our home several times for dinner. In fact, Lily already asked him to join us for *this* Christmas Eve, but he declined, giving the same excuse (busy, busy) as last year. I think he's seen *Miracle on 34th Street* one too many times!

I sometimes wonder if he's given any thought to suing for false arrest regarding the poor box incident. Probably not. Been there, done that.

What Lily wants this year for Christmas is more of a challenge than last year's gift. Want the truth? I wouldn't mind a 'do-over' of last year's adventure. I'm secretly hoping she'll meet another Santa in need and once again ask for my help as her Christmas gift. That would be easier than giving her what she's currently demanding to make her Christmas merry—a tattoo and a belly button ring. Yikes!

Copyright ©2007 Gail Farrelly

The Proper Trimmings

Nick Andreychuk

The first thing Russ noticed when Anna opened her apartment door was the comforting smell of Christmas dinner. The mouth-watering aroma of roasted turkey assaulted him, momentarily knocking him senseless. Then he noticed Anna. Wearing a short red skirt and a tight green blouse, she was even more of a babe than he'd imagined.

Anna smiled knowingly, and guided Russ to a cloth-covered card table next to a haphazardly decorated Christmas tree in the middle of an otherwise empty dining room. A fresh loaf of bread was already on the table. Russ tore off a chunk without saying hello.

"Wine?" Anna asked.

"Rum and eggnog," Russ grunted through a mouthful of bread.

Anna winked at him, went to the adjoining kitchen, and returned with a large thermos full of warm holiday cheer.

Russ couldn't believe his luck. This chick was just his type; she even looked a little like his last girlfriend. While writing Anna from prison, he'd fantasized that she would be an obedient looker, but deep down he'd expected her to be some lonely loser who couldn't do any better than a man behind bars. She'd said in her letters that she believed in helping those who couldn't help themselves.

Tonight, he intended to avail himself of whatever "help" she planned to offer. This was the night he'd dreamed about for ten long years.

Anna had never mentioned a boyfriend in her letters, and she wasn't wearing a wedding ring, but Russ wanted to be sure anyway. "Now that I see what you look like," he said, "I'm kinda surprised you had any free time to write."

"What a sweet thing to say. Truth is, I find writing letters therapeutic," she said. "I used to live in Europe, and my sister and I corresponded weekly. She was an ER nurse, so her schedule was too erratic for phone calls. We stayed close through letters... But she died unexpectedly, and it left a hole in my life. I guess I filled that hole partly through writing you."

Great, Russ thought. *She's needy and lonely, and she thinks she needs therapy.*

A timer went off. "Turkey's ready," Anna said. She went to the kitchen and returned with the bird on a big platter, surrounded by roasted potatoes and vegetables, with homemade stuffing spilling out of it.

"Mmm-mmm." Russ practically drooled over Anna's hand as she set the platter in front of him. While he carved the turkey, Anna made another quick trip to the kitchen and the smell of gravy soon permeated the room. "I've been looking forward to this for a long time," he said.

Anna smiled. "I know. A girl could get a complex worrying about getting your mama's stuffing recipe just right."

"Sorry if I came off as picky in my letters, but when you haven't eaten your favorite dish for so long..." Russ shrugged.

"Don't worry. I understand how important this meal is to you. Still, I'd reckon you've always been picky about your mama's recipe, even before you— Y'know, you never *did* tell me what you were in for..."

Russ glanced down. "We should eat this while it's hot," he said. "We'll talk later, okay?"

"Sure," Anna said, as she sat down across from him. "I'm not much of a meat eater, but you go ahead and dig in."

"You don't know what you're missing," Russ said. After he filled his plate, he took a heaping spoonful of turkey, stuffing, and gravy, and savored it in his mouth like it was a fine wine. "Darlin,' you got the magic touch. I think I'm in love."

Russ thought he saw a look of discomfort cross Anna's face when he mentioned the word "love," but it disappeared so quickly that he figured it was just his lingering doubts about a hottie being interested in him.

"I'm glad you like it," Anna said with a smile. "I made some substitutions to the stuffing, and I worried you'd notice."

Russ ate another mouthful. "Nope, can't tell about no substitutions. Maybe it's 'cause it's been so long, or maybe it's 'cause you make a livin' cooking. No matter, 'cause this is *good*."

Russ shoveled down the rest of the food on his plate in one minute flat.

"Care for more?" Anna asked.

"Sure thing, sweet thing."

Russ downed a glass of rum and eggnog, then poured himself another, before filling his plate higher than the first time.

Anna sipped a glass of wine and watched with a serene look while Russ ate with unrelenting gusto. *She must really get off on people enjoying her cooking*, he thought.

The second Russ dropped his fork onto his empty plate, Anna put down her glass and said, "Can I ask you something?"

"Sure."

"Now that you're out, and you've had your special meal, it's time you told me what you did to get ten years of hard time."

Russ gulped down some more spiked eggnog, then said, "Yeah, I guess we need to get this out of the way with. And now that *you* have nothin' to worry about, I can tell ya... I accidentally killed my last girlfriend, Rachel."

Anna's voice shook as she responded, "*Accidentally?*"

"Yeah, well, she uh, kept screwin' up my mama's recipe, and the last time she made it for me was the worst ever. I kinda lost my temper and shoved some of the crap down her throat—only my fork pierced somethin' and she wound up dead. I felt bad and all, but it *was* an accident and I don't even think I should've done *any* time..."

"You're right," Anna said. "You didn't deserve to go to prison."

Russ was flabbergasted. "You don't think I deserved to do time?"

"No. All you wanted was to be able to eat your traditional holiday meal, and now you've gotten *exactly* what you deserve."

Something in her voice made him shudder. Then he coughed, and the next thing he knew, he was hacking up a lung. *What the—*

"Oh my," Anna said. "Are you okay?" Her concern sounded over-exaggerated.

"No," Russ coughed, "I'm *not okay*! Get me some water or somethin'."

"I wonder if it's my stuffing. The substitutions? Do you have any allergies?"

"Yes! I wrote them in my last letter."

"Oh, I got rid of all those letters you sent me."

"What? Why?" Russ grasped his throat in pain and fell off his chair. His face turned blue, and his lips swelled up to the size of bananas.

He managed to gasp out a few more words. "Help me...*please*."

"I'm sorry, I'm just the **cook** in my family. My sister *Rachel* was **the one** with medical training..."

Copyright ©2007 Nick Andreychuk

The Grinch And I
Herschel Cozine

George took the job as Santa Claus for the Holman Mall in spite of the pay—minimum wage, with two thirty minute, unpaid breaks a day. He fit the part: short, overweight, in his sixties. A fake beard and square glasses, along with the red suit with faux fur, made him a perfect Santa. And the work was easy, mostly sitting, posing for the camera while kids of all ages climbed on his knee and screamed for their mothers. The candy cane he gave them usually quieted them down, but there were always a few in the course of a day who made him wish he had chosen another line of work.

George didn't take the job for the money, of course, or for the privilege of giving out candy canes to ungrateful, squalling kids. The reason was simple: it was the perfect cover for his line of work. George was a shoplifter.

During his breaks, George was free to go into any shop without being questioned or scrutinized by clerks or security. He was met with friendly smiles, a season greeting, and a wave of the hand. There is something about a Santa Claus suit that elicits trust. Santa Claus is beloved by all, no matter who is in the suit.

And the bag he carried made it easy to store items he would never be able to take otherwise. He had quick hands, a requirement for his profession. With a flick of the hand an item was transferred from the display case to his coat pocket. The size of the loot had to be within the limits of his pocket. Even with loose fitting shirts and coats, the booty could not be too large, or the telltale bulge could result in an arrest. He had learned this the hard way years ago. But now, with the bag, he was able to walk away with larger, more desirable merchandise.

So George, the shoplifting Santa, was happy in his work—at least the part where he wasn't dealing with kids and parents. His only regret was that he hadn't thought of it sooner. Just think of the money he could have saved on Christmas presents over the years. Well, this year he would be more than generous with his gift giving. Unmarried, he nevertheless had siblings, nephews, nieces, and an aged father to buy for. He might even throw in a watch or apron for his landlady. The old witch could use some softening up. She was threatening to raise the rent, and George would have to look for another place to live if she did. He was not a wealthy man. Shoplifting didn't pay the rent.

The first few days on the job, George limited his break time to "casing the joint". That way the clerks and security personnel would become accustomed to his presence and leave him to his nefarious activity. And, as Christmas neared, the stores became more crowded, offering him further protection from unwanted prying eyes.

His first foray was at Penney's. In the course of ten minutes he had appropriated a pair of Deerfoam slippers, (size 10, his father's size), two packages of socks, and a necktie for his younger brother. He ambled out of the store with his sack over his shoulder, waved cheerfully to the clerk behind the men's clothing counter and wished him a Merry Christmas. He ignored the man in the dark suit who was dutifully studying the hosiery rack, pretending to be a customer. Gilbert, longtime security man for J.C. Penney's, stood out like a sore thumb. George had developed an instinct over the years to spot and avoid men like Gilbert.

At Macy's, George visited the cookware department where he found a set of carving knives. He looked up and down the aisle. An older couple was engaged in a spirited conversation, apparently over which frying pan to buy. A few feet in the other direction was a man busily talking on a cell phone. George smiled at the irony of it. Cell phones keep one connected to a far away voice while isolating him from someone standing a few feet away. With a deft sleight of hand, George became the owner of the knives.

By the end of his second week on the job, George had gifts for everyone in the family. He was particularly proud of the gift he had "purchased" for Grover, his six year old grandnephew. A fire truck, complete with siren, flashing lights and a hose that squirted water. Grover had admired it on an earlier trip to the mall, and had even asked George to get it for him. Of course, he didn't realize he was asking his uncle. He was sitting on his lap at the mall when the request was made. George had given him a candy cane, patted him on the head, and promised him that he would grant his wish if he would be a good boy for the next four weeks. This, he knew, would be a daunting task for Grover, but the incentive was great enough to give it a try. Grover swallowed hard and nodded, but the look in his eyes told George that he was hoping Santa would be too busy to keep tabs on him. A chip off the old block, George noted fondly as he watched him walk away. He determined he would get the fire truck. It was the least he could do for his favorite relative.

    It was a week before Christmas. George had stolen enough wrapping paper to take care of all the gifts. He had completed the task of wrapping and tagging, and had carefully stored the gifts under his bed where they would stay until Christmas Eve. He fixed a glass of eggnog, fortified it with a touch of rum, and kicked off his shoes. The TV was showing "A Christmas Carol", one of the many versions of Dickens' classic, starring Albert Finney. In George's mind, it was the best of the lot. He settled back in his recliner, avoiding the broken spring. Some day he would buy a new chair, since it was impossible, even for a man of his talent, to shoplift one.

Christmas Future had just exited, leaving a transformed Scrooge to dance around in his nightgown, when the doorbell rang. George sighed and stood up. Glancing at the TV as he walked to the door, he opened it to see a total stranger standing on the other side.

"Mister Grimes?" the man said.

George studied the man a moment before answering. Medium build, ordinary face, brown short cropped hair, he wouldn't draw a second look in a crowd. Yet he looked vaguely familiar.

"Who are you?" George replied. "What do you want?"

"My name is Pierce. Stanley Pierce. May I come in?"

"Not until you tell me what you want." George growled.

"Of course," Pierce said amiably. "It concerns your job at the mall. Santa."

"What about it?"

"Please, sir," Pierce said in a low voice. "It would be better if we talked inside. I don't think you would want the neighbors to hear what I have to say."

George scowled at the man, then stepped aside and let him in.

"This better be good," he said.

Pierce surveyed the room with a hint of disapproval, but said nothing. Gesturing toward a chair, he said, "May I?"

"Yeah. Go ahead. Sit."

Pierce sat down gingerly, as if the chair contained snakes, surveyed the room a second time, his eyes finally settling on George. "This is a matter of utmost importance," he said.

George returned the man's gaze but said nothing. He had learned that silence was a virtue for a man in his profession.

"How should I start?" Pierce asked. Then, before George could speak, he went on. "I'm an employee of Holman's Mall. Security."

The word startled George and he sat up straight.

"When you were hired, I did a background check," Pierce went on. "Routine, you know." He took a paper from his pocket, unfolded it and studied it through his bifocals. "In 1979 you were convicted of shoplifting in Santa Fe, and served thirty days." He glanced at George with an apologetic smile. George met his gaze in silence.

Pierce cleared his throat and went on. "In 1984 you were charged with petty larceny—shoplifting—in Phoenix. The charges were dropped when you made restitution." Another smile, less apologetic. "These charges raised a red flag, and I decided to keep an eye on you."

George shifted in his chair and scowled at Pierce. "That was a long time ago. I made a few mistakes. Nobody's perfect."

"Agreed. But given your history it seemed prudent to monitor your activities." A meaningful glance made George squirm. He could see where this was going and he didn't want to go there.

Pierce folded the paper and put it back in his pocket. Extracting another paper, he repeated the process of unfolding and studying it. "On Wednesday, three weeks ago, you visited Penney's. While there you acquired some merchandise without paying for it. To be specific, one pair of Deerfoam slippers, two packages of socks, and a necktie."

George started to protest, but Pierce stopped him with a raised hand. "At 'Mark's Apparel, Etc.', you lifted a watch, sweatshirt—X Large—and several packets of handkerchiefs."

"I don't..." George sputtered.

"Please, sir," Pierce said quietly. "Let me continue."

"No," George said. "I've heard enough." He studied Pierce with a professional eye. "I don't remember seeing you around. I can't believe you were following me."

Pierce smiled. "You're good, Mister Grimes. Very good. But so am I. Avoiding detection is as important to my profession as it is to yours."

"So," George said with a sigh, "what now? Are you turning me in? Why didn't you do something at the time?"

"I had my reasons," Pierce said. "Are you willing to make a deal?"

"What kind of deal."

Pierce looked around the room furtively. "I am a fairminded man. And a compassionate one. You see, each Christmas I find a family in need and help them. A present or two to each member. A bag of groceries. And a turkey for their Christmas dinner." He cleared his throat and sat up straight. "This is all done anonymously."

How noble, George thought, but said nothing.

"I'm a man of modest means. As you can see, this can be expensive. I must depend on donations in order to continue this effort."

"Donations?" George let the word slip off his tongue with an edge of sarcasm.

Pierce ignored the inflection and nodded. "The Marines have 'Toys For Tots', a very worthwhile endeavor. But I like to think that my way is a little more personal, if not as far reaching. It does my heart such good to see the family I helped enjoy a Christmas that would otherwise be difficult." A sigh, somewhere between contentment and regret, escaped his lips. "But, alas. I must rely on people such as yourself to continue."

"You want the loot," George said.

"A rather indelicate way of phrasing it, but, yes. All donations gratefully accepted."

"How much of it?"

"Oh, all of it, of course."

George stood up angrily. "No way! I worked hard for that and I got people of my own to take care of. I'll give you half."

Pierce's laugh was without humor. "Mister Grimes, you don't appreciate the position you are in. A word from me and you are facing serious jail time. This is no longer petty theft. By my accounting you have taken over one thousand dollars in merchandise."

"You'd look bad reporting me at this late date," George said. "You're in this as deep as I am."

"On the contrary," Pierce replied. "An anonymous phone call to my supervisor. He would ask me to look into it. A surprise visit to your home, and..." He held up the list.

George snorted. "It's too late for that. You can't prove I didn't pay for the stuff. It's in my house and I don't need receipts. Hell, who keeps receipts once they get the stuff home?"

"Oh, I anticipated that," Pierce said smugly. He reached into his coat pocket and pulled out a cell phone.

"These gadgets come in handy," he said. "They allow you to talk to anyone no matter where you may be. Like Macy's for example."

"I don't understand," George said.

"They also take pictures." Pierce pressed a button and held the phone out for George to see.

"Recognize anyone?" Pierce said.

George flushed as he looked at himself

putting a set of carving knives in his bag. He reached for the phone, but Pierce pulled it away.

"You were the guy talking on the phone." George swore under his breath.

"I wasn't really talking on the phone at all. I was waiting for you to make your move, knowing you had decided that I was just another harried shopper. As I said, Mister Grimes, avoiding detection is important in my profession."

George swore again. How could he have been fooled by such a transparent trick? He had learned how to deal with security cameras by carefully positioning himself so his movements could not be recorded. But cell phones were something new. He hadn't considered their versatility. He hadn't kept up with the times.

George sighed with resignation and sat down. "Eighty-twenty," he said.

Another shake of the head.

"Let me keep the wallet," George said.

"Wallet?" Pierce studied the list and frowned. "That's not on my list. You must have taken that on a Tuesday—my day off."

George thought fast. It had been Tuesday, the same day he had stolen the fire truck for Grover. How fortuitous! Trying to hide his relief, he shrugged.

"OK. You win." He crossed to the bed in the corner of the room and removed the wrapped gifts from under it, careful to leave the fire truck back against the wall and out of sight.

"My family will be most grateful for your generosity, Mister Grimes."

"Yeah," George said. "Now. Get rid of the picture."

Pierce paused and considered the request. Then with a shrug, he pushed a button and the picture was gone.

"Satisfied?" he said.

George grunted.

Pierce collected the gifts and placed them in a sack he had brought with him, tied it and flung it over his back. He grunted under the weight. "Now I know how you feel," he said patting the sack. "Good night." He paused in the doorway and turned to George.

"Merry Christmas."

George shut the door hard, catching Pierce in the rearend. He locked it, took a swig of eggnog and sat down. *Parasite!* George, fuming over his misfortune, cursed the man.

"Needy family my arse" George growled. He was willing to bet there wasn't a family, that Pierce was keeping the loot for himself.

George glared at the TV, where the Grinch was tying his dog, Max, to the sleigh. Christmas! Humbug!

Then he smiled in spite of himself. At least Grover wouldn't be disappointed. He was probably home this very minute trying to be good. Unsuccessfully, George was certain.

But the effort was worthy of reward. Well, he would have his fire truck, thanks to George's good fortune.

And tomorrow George would start his Christmas shopping all over again. But not at Holman's Mall. Walmart was just down the street. And George knew all the security guards by name. He would steer clear of shoppers with cell phones, too. Of course, he would have to limit the size of the gifts to fit his pocket, no longer having the benefit of Santa's sack. Ah, well. Such is life. He held the glass of eggnog up to the TV in a salute to the Grinch. After all, they had a lot in common. They both stole for Christmas, and they both gave it back.

"Skoal," he said cheerfully. He didn't know what it meant, but he meant it. Every word.

Copyright ©2007 Herschel Cozine

Home for Christmas

A River City Short Story
Frank Zafiro

"Why can't you come home for Christmas?"

It seemed to Detective Katie MacLeod that her mother injected as much guilt-inspiring tone into her voice as possible through the telephone line.

And the booze, she thought.

She sighed. "Mom—"

"Don't sigh at me."

Katie sighed again, but then apologized. "Look, Mom, someone has to work it."

"Why? It's Christmas!"

"Police work is a twenty-four seven business. Crime doesn't take a holiday."

"That's ridiculous."

"We have to have a detective on duty. And if no one with seniority takes it, then it ends up being the low guy."

"You can't still be the newest detective after three years," her mother said

"Well, no," Katie admitted. "But I volunteered because they all have families."

"And you don't! What do you call me?"

"Families with spouses and kids, Mom. You know, kids? Little ones who wouldn't understand why Daddy has to work on Christmas?"

Her mother snorted. "Well, that's

87

just...well..."

"It is what it is," Katie said. "Look, I drew the first twelve hours. Six in the morning to six at night. As long as nothing happens, I can be over there by midnight."

"That's not even Christmas anymore," her mother huffed. "Besides, you can't drive. The passes are shut down except for four wheel drives with chains. You'd have to fly to get here."

"So I'll catch a flight on the 26th. It'll be easy. No one else will be traveling that day."

"That's because all normal people are with their families."

"Mom—"

"Just do what's important to you," her mother snapped and hung up.

Katie stared at the handset for a long moment. Then she lowered it onto the cradle, shaking her head.

'Tis the season, she thought.

***

She showed up at ten of six with a Hazelnut latte and the newspaper. The lights flickered and hummed when she hit the switch, casting wavering light down on the empty desks in the bullpen.

Katie hung her coat, dropped the paper onto her desk and switched on the computer. After booting up, she checked email. All that was new were a couple of generic administrative messages. She deleted them.

The rustle of the newspaper seemed loud in the empty room. She read and sipped her latte.

She'd worked her way through everything but the sports page and the classified when her phone rang. She snatched the receiver, grateful at the prospect of human contact.

"Detective MacLeod."

"Merry Christmas, girl." Detective John Tower's voice boomed in the earpiece.

Katie pulled the phone away from her ear momentarily. "Sheesh, John. Blow out my eardrums, why don't you?"

Tower lowered his voice. "Sorry."

"It's all right."

Tower paused, then cleared his throat. "Anyway, I just thought I'd give you a call. You know, to say Merry Christmas."

"Thanks."

"So, uh, Merry Christmas."

"Merry Christmas, John."

"Is it busy?"

"Two robberies and a serious assault already this morning," she said.

"What? You serious?"

"Absolutely. I only just came back to get some more crime scene tape."

"Oh, man. You need some help? I can call Browning, or maybe Finch and Elias. We could—"

"Relax, John," Katie said. "I'm just kidding. It's quiet. No calls."

Tower didn't reply. Finally, he said, "Really?"

"Really. I'm about to do the crossword."

"Well, eight across is probably 'gullible.'" Tower chuckled. "You got me, girl."

Katie smiled.

"Anyway," Tower said. "Have a good shift. And if it gets too busy, you can call me. Ben will have these presents torn apart before ten. After that, I'm available if you need anything."

"Thanks."

Tower hung up.

Katie read the sports page and scanned the classifieds. Then she broke out a pen and began work on the crossword. When she realized eight across was 'infatuated,' she allowed herself a long chuckle.

By noon, she'd played too many games of solitaire and was officially bored.

At one-thirty, the phone rang again.

"Detective MacLeod."

"Merry Christmas," came a woman's bright voice. "This is Janice in Dispatch. Are you interested in helping patrol out with a call?"

"Definitely."

Janice gave her the details. She scrawled them into her notebook and hung up with a thank you and a Merry Christmas. Coat in hand, she strode out of the police station. Five minutes later, she was parking in front of an ATM across the street from her destination. A marked patrol car sat directly in front of the business.

Officer Jack Willow waited for her at the glass door entrance to the small business suite. He briefed her without preamble. "The owner came down to pick up some presents for his wife that he had hidden in his office. Found the door unlocked and the safe empty."

Katie examined the door and saw no damage. "Is this the only way in?"

Willow nodded. "Yeah. And there's no forced entry."

"Did he forget to lock up?"

"No." Willow shook his head. "In fact, he is adamant about that."

Willow led her through the door and into the small office. Katie glanced around and saw no signs of ransacking.

Aside from the main office area, there was only one private office. That was where Willow took her. Inside, a middle-aged man sat at the opulent desk, his head in his hands.

"Mr. Burnwell?" Willow said.

The man looked up. His eyes were red and bleary and his hair askew from sleep. The jeans and T-shirt looked out of character on him, almost as if he were wearing a costume.

"This is the detective," Willow told him.

"Oh, thank heavens," Burnwell said, rising to stand.

Katie held out her hand and Burnwell shook it. His palms were damp but his grip sure.

"Are you going to find my money?" he asked.

"I'm going to try," Katie told him. "Can you tell me what happened?"

Burnwell's eyes flicked to Willow and back to her. "I already told him. I'd hate to think we're wasting time here."

Katie gave him a warm smile. "It's not a waste. I just need to know the facts before I can begin my investigation."

Burnwell sighed. "Well, of course. That makes sense, I suppose." He sighed again and sat back down heavily into his overstuffed chair. With his hand, he motioned toward the wall. "I've been cleaned out."

Katie followed his motion to the empty, open safe on the wall. "And you discovered the money missing this morning?"

"About an hour ago," he said.

"How much?"

"All of it."

"Do you have actual figures?" Katie asked.

Burnwell shrugged. "Eventually, after the season, we'll figure it all out. But I'm guessing a hundred, maybe a hundred and fifty."

"Thousand?"

Burnwell nodded.

"Why was that much in your safe?"

"The vendors brought it in last night."

"Vendors?"

Burnwell nodded again. "Yes. Detective, do you even know what business I'm in?"

"No," Katie admitted, feeling foolish even though she had no reason to. "Why don't you fill me in?"

Burnwell drew himself up in his seat. "Are you familiar with those kiosks in the mall? The seasonal ones?"

"I think so. They sell Christmas stuff?"

"Not just Christmas items. Remote control cars, sunglasses, jewelry, you name it. I have seven carts between the two malls. We do eighty percent of our yearly business in the month of December. Much of it is in cash."

"And the vendors brought in the cash on Christmas Eve?"

"Yes. The last week's worth, anyway. I put it in the safe."

"Why not the bank?"

"The banks were all closed by the time they closed up shop at nine o'clock. I planned on depositing the money the day after Christmas when the banks open back up."

Katie nodded in understanding. "Who else has access to the office?"

"Just my two employees."

"None of the vendors?"

"No."

Katie flipped open her notebook. "What are the names of your employees?"

"Carla Stehr is the accountant," Burnwell said. "And Jeri Nives is the receptionist. But I don't think they—"

"Did they both have access to the safe as well?" Katie asked him.

"Well...yes."

Katie snapped the notebook shut. "Then I'll need to talk to them." She glanced around the room. "Did you get what you came for this morning?"

"Huh?"

"Your wife's presents?"

"Oh." Burnwell nodded. "Yeah, they're in the car."

Katie excused herself and returned to her police car. She considered calling out Forensics to photograph and print the scene, but dismissed the idea. The photos would be simple ones that she could take with her digital camera. And prints really didn't matter. Both suspects' fingerprints would be all over the office, including the safe. It wouldn't prove anything.

She returned to Burnwell's office and snapped a dozen shots, though she realized it was probably overkill. When she'd finished, she asked Burnwell, "Where will you be the remainder of the day?"

"I'm going back home to be with my wife," he said. "Will you call me if you find out anything?"

"I will."

***

Jeri Nives lived in a large apartment complex. Katie eventually found the building with the right letter on it, but it took another five minutes until she stood in front of the right apartment number.

No one answered her repeated knocks. She graduated from polite taps to loud pounds, but no one came to the door. She gave it one last try with the butt end of her flashlight before giving up.

The door across from Jeri's opened up. "What's the racket?"

Katie turned to the man. He looked to be in his forties, wore glasses and a drooping mustache. She held up her badge. "You know Jeri Nives?"

"Sure. She in trouble?"

"I just need to talk to her. Do you know where she is?"

"Went to her Mom's house, I think."

"Did she tell you that?"

"Yeah. I ran into her when I got the paper. I invited her over for eggnog, but she said she couldn't because she was going to her mother's house."

"Do you know where that is?"

He shook his head. "Sorry, I don't."

"All right." She handed him a business card. "Thanks. Sorry for disturbing you."

"No worries..." He glanced down at the card. "Katie. You want to come in for some eggnog?"

She smiled. "Sorry, can't. Working."

"Okay, then. Well, Merry Christmas."

***

She had better luck at Carla Stehr's house. Through the glass windows in the front door, she saw a woman in her fifties watching television. Katie knocked.

Carla answered the door. "Yes?"

Katie showed her badge. "Can I come in and talk with you for a minute?"

"Of course." Carla opened the door wide and let her in.

Five minutes later, the two women were seat at the small dining room table sipping tea that Carla insisted on making.

Katie opened her notebook and took down Carla's basic biographical information. Then she said, "Do you have any idea why I'm here, Mrs. Stehr?"

Carla shook her head.

"Your office was broken into. Some money was stolen." Katie watched her reaction carefully.

Carla's eyebrows flew up in surprise. "Was anyone hurt?"

"No. No one was there when it happened."

"What was taken?"

"Money from the safe."

Carla's eyes widened further. "The money from the safe?"

"Yes. Do you know how much that would be?"

"Not exactly, no. Mr. Burnwell collected it from the vendors all day long. I knew he wasn't going to make it to the bank before it closed." She shook her head in amazement. "There must have been over a hundred thousand in that safe."

"You're the accountant? Do you count the money before it goes to the bank?"

"No. I usually deal with the bank receipts when I balance the books."

"Do you have any idea who could have done this?"

She considered. "Well, obviously, it would have to be someone with access to the safe."

"Who has that access."

"Mr. Burnwell, Jeri and myself."

"No one else?"

"Not that I know of. Maybe Mrs. Burnwell, but I doubt it."

"Why?"

"She's...a little bit on the simple side," Carla said. "If it isn't socializing or shopping, she's not too interested.

"A trophy wife?"

"Oh, that's such a horrible description," Carla answered. "But yes, I suppose so."

"So between Jeri and Mr. Burnwell, who do you think could have taken the money?"

Carla raised her hand to her mouth. "Oh, I couldn't say. I mean, to accuse somebody—"

"I'm not asking for an accusation, Mrs. Stehr. Just your thoughts."

Carla looked down at her teacup. "I

don't know about taking money," she said carefully. "But I'm pretty sure the two of them were carrying on, if you know what I mean."

"An affair?"

"Something like that." Carla looked up. "I don't have any proof, mind you. Just my impression, based on how they behave around each other."

"Did this affair start or stop recently?"

"Oh, no," Carla said. "It's been going on for most of the year, I'd guess."

"Do you know where Jeri's mother lives?"

"I do. I dropped her off once." She gave Katie the address.

"One last thing," Katie asked. "Did you take the money, Carla?"

Carla brought her hands to her chest. "Heavens, no!"

"Would you be willing to take a polygraph exam?"

"A lie detector?"

Katie nodded.

Carla pressed her lips together. Her hands shook slightly. "Well, I suppose. If it were necessary."

Katie rose from her seat. "Thank you, Mrs. Stehr. And thanks for the tea."

***

Jeri wasn't at her mother's house. And her mother, Pauline, wasn't happy about it.

"You'd think a daughter would want to spend Christmas with the woman who brought her into the world," she groused.

"Do you know where she is?" Katie asked, ignoring the editorial comment.

"I have no idea. If I did, I'd be giving her an earful, believe me you!"

Katie handed her a business card. "If she comes back, would you have her give me a call?"

Pauline took the card, but didn't look at it. "I wouldn't get your hopes up, missy. She won't even call her own mother."

***

Katie drove back to the station and sat at her desk. She thought things over for a bit, absently chewing on her nails as she tossed the case over in her mind. A picture was starting to form. The problem was that she didn't know enough to know if it was the right picture or not.

She reached for the telephone and called Burnwell's house. On the fourth ring, a woman answered.

"Mrs. Burnwell?"

"Yes. Who's this?"

"Detective MacLeod. I'm investigating the burglary at your husband's business."

"Oh. Is that finished yet? Because I was hoping to go out for dinner tonight."

Katie paused. "Mr. Burnwell isn't back yet?"

"No. He said the police needed him for a while yet. Are you almost finished?"

"Almost," Katie said. "I do have a couple of questions for you, though."

"Me?"

"Yes. Does your husband have a cell phone?"

"Of course."

"Can you give me the number?"

Mrs. Burnwell recited it from memory. "What was your other question?"

"Did you enjoy the gifts your husband bought for you this year?"

"What kind of question is that?"

"I'm just curious. When did you open them?"

"This morning. But what does that—

"Thank you, Mrs. Burnwell."

Katie hung up and dialed the cell number. It rang six times and went to voicemail. She left a message asking Burnwell to call her.

The picture seemed clearer, but she wasn't sure yet. She let the ideas simmer in her head while she ran all three of the principals through the computer. None of them had any entries worth noting.

Katie looked up at the ceiling. "So the husband and the secretary took the stash and lit out for Mexico or something?"

Could be. But the problem was that it really wasn't that much money. Enough to steal, sure, but hardly enough to run away on.

And why would he call it in if he was planning to run?

It didn't make sense.

Her phone rang. She grabbed the receiver. "Detective MacLeod."

"Uh, hey, this is Joe. From the apartments earlier?"

"Oh, right. The eggnog."

"Exactly!"

"What can I do for you, Joe?"

"I was just wondering. You're sure Jeri isn't in any kind of trouble?"

"I just need to talk to her."

"Okay, then. Well, she's home now." His voice dropped a few decibels. "Her and some older guy."

***

Katie didn't exactly run code to get to Jeri's apartment, but she definitely broke a few traffic laws. She parked her car and took the stairs two at a time. At Jeri's door, she paused a moment to catch her breath, then knocked.

No answer came for several moments. Then a female voice asked through the door, "Who is it?"

Katie held her badge up to the peephole. "River City Police, Jeri. I need to talk to you."

There was a pause, then the rattling of a chain as Jeri opened the door. A woman in her mid-twenties with a flowing mane of blond hair stood in the doorway. Katie took in her perfect curves with a twinge of jealousy.

"What's this about?" Jeri demanded.

"You mind if I come in?"

Jeri hesitated, then opened the door wider. Katie stepped inside. Her gaze swept the living room. It was decorated with crystal figurines and new age paintings. A bright white loveseat dominated the room.

"Where is he?" Katie asked.

"Who?"

Katie turned to her and gave her a tight

smile. "Let's not play games, Jeri. Where's your boss?"

"At home, I imagine." She crossed her arms and affected a haughty demeanor. "It is Christmas."

"No, he's here," Katie said. "Now why don't you go get him and let's work things out."

Jeri paused, returning Katie's stare. The women engaged in a brief battle of wills before Jeri looked away with a sneer. Then she stomped into the bedroom. Katie heard her speak in a muffled voice. A few moments later, she emerged from the bedroom with Burnwell in tow. The man gave Katie a sheepish look.

"Detective. Uh, any news on the case?"

Katie pointed to the white couch. Burnwell sat down meekly. Jeri snorted at them both and plopped onto the couch next to him, crossing her arms and legs in a huff.

"Let me tell you what I know, Mr. Burnwell." Katie fixed him with a matter-of-fact stare. "For starters, I know that you have been having an affair with Jeri here for the better part of a year."

"It's not an affair," Jeri snapped. "We're in love."

Katie ignored her. "I also know that you didn't come down to the office to get presents for your wife. She opened them earlier this morning."

Burnwell opened his mouth to reply,

then closed it.

"You want to tell me what you came down to the office for, Mr. Burnwell?"

"I...came to get a little cash."

"From the safe."

He nodded glumly. "I was going to take Jeri to a nice restaurant for Christmas. And I had to pick up her presents, too."

Jeri drew her hair back to display a pair of diamond earrings. "Beautiful, aren't they?"

Katie continued to ignore her. "What did you do with the rest of the money?"

Burnwell looked confused. "The rest? I don't understand."

"I think you do. What did you do with the rest of the money from the safe?"

Burnwell shook his head. "There was no money. It was gone."

"Gone?"

Jeri smacked her gum and turned to Burnwell. "She's not very smart for a detective."

Burnwell cleared his throat. "All the money was already gone when I got there."

Katie's eyes bored into him. "Are you sure?"

"Of course."

"Would you take a polygraph exam?"

"Of course."

"How about you?" Katie asked Jeri.

The blond woman looked at Katie with a put-upon expression. "A what?"

"A lie detector," Burnwell told her.

103

Jeri shrugged and smacked her gum again. "Sure. Why not?"

Katie took a deep breath and sighed. "Why didn't you tell me this before?" she asked Burnwell.

Burnwell looked over at Jeri. The blond woman sat bouncing her leg over her knee and smacking her gum impatiently. Burnwell looked back at Katie and shrugged.

"Discretion?" he said in a meek voice.

***

Carla Stehr opened the door with a pleasant hello. "Did you find Jeri at her mother's house?" she asked Katie when they'd settled at the dining room table again.

Katie shook her head. "No. But I found Jeri."

"Well, that's good."

"I found out everything, actually."

"Good," Carla repeated.

"You need to tell me where the money is, Carla."

"I'm sure I don't know."

"You do," Katie said. "Unfortunately, you do."

Carla took on a miffed expression. "It's not very polite to accuse people, detective. Particularly on Christmas. Now, perhaps—"

"You know there's an ATM across the street from the office?"

Carla paused. "Yes," she said slowly. "I've used it once or twice."

"You know where that camera points?"

Carla didn't answer.

"It points right at the front of the business. When I go to the bank tomorrow and pull the tape from that camera, you know what I'll see?" Katie leaned forward. "I'll see you pull up in your car and go inside. I'll see you leave with a bag of some kind."

"No," Carla whispered.

"Yes, I will," Katie told her. "And if I search your house right now, I will find that bag in your closet or in the attic or maybe in the laundry room. And in your bedroom, I'll find your suitcase on the bed, half-packed. Won't I, Carla?"

The older woman didn't reply.

Katie continued. "After I do all of those things, it doesn't much matter what you say or do. It does matter now, though. It matters if you're honest about things. It matters if you return the money."

Carla brought her shaking fingers to her face and bowed her head.

"Why'd you do it, Carla?"

Carla's shoulders hitched and she let out a whimper.

"Tell me," Katie urged.

Carla looked up at her, tears filling her eyes. "All that money," she whispered. "Every year, all that money. All that cash. A lot more than he tells anyone. I know he skims bunches of it before it goes to the bank. And what he doesn't skim, he keeps for himself. Spends it on his trophy wife and the trophy girlfriend.

Big, extravagant gifts, I'm sure."

An image of Jeri's diamond earrings flashed through Katie's mind.

"Do you know what he got me this year?" Carla asked. She pointed to the kitchen counter at a bottle of wine. "Twenty dollars from the grocery store, I'd bet. And I don't even drink alcohol."

"So he doesn't appreciate you?"

Carla laughed and wiped her tears away. "Oh, honey, he doesn't even hardly know me. And he only appreciates one thing about women. Do you think he puts any of that money into a retirement fund for any of us?"

"Probably not."

"I'm all alone," Carla told her. "It's just me. Do you know what it's like to be alone?"

"I do." Katie swallowed. "So you took the money."

Carla nodded. "It was going to be my retirement. It's not like I can count on Social Security."

***

Katie booked Carla into jail without incident. Everyone in the booking area, corrections officers and criminals alike, looked at her like she was a giant Scrooge. She was glad to get out of there.

She logged the money onto the property book. She could have returned the money to Burnwell with a property receipt, but she decided to make him come down to the property room the next day so it could be counted out for him. It was evidence, after all, and she didn't like the idea of him using the money for an expensive dinner with Jeri. Let him use a credit card.

Back at her desk, Katie typed her report. After all of her work, she was surprised at how brief the actual narrative looked. She printed it off and put it in a file. By the time she finished, it was seven-thirty. Detective Bill Lindsay had arrived at six and was busy whistling off-key Christmas songs at his own desk.

Katie picked up the phone and dialed. Her mother picked up on the fourth ring.

"Mom?"

"Is that Katie?" her mother slurred.

"It's me," Katie said quietly, not wanting Lindsay to hear. "I just wanted to wish you Merry Christmas."

Her mother barked out a laugh. "Oh, it's Merry all right. Merry, merry, merry. All by my merry self."

"I'm sorry I had to work."

"Your whole life is sorry," came the slurred accusation.

"You don't mean that, Mom."

"What do you know what I mean?" she said stubbornly.

Katie heard her sip from a glass. Or maybe a bottle. "I'll catch a flight tomorrow," she promised.

"Don't bother yourself," her mother muttered and hung up the phone.

Katie lowered the receiver onto the cradle. Tears sprang up in her eyes. Lindsay whistled, butchering "Jingle Bells."

Without thinking, Katie picked up the phone and dialed Tower's number. He answered on the second ring.

"John? It's Katie."

"Hey, girl. Merry Christmas."

"Thanks."

"You still at work?"

"Just finishing up."

"Who's the idiot whistling in the background?"

"Lindsay."

Tower chuckled. "I should've guessed."

"Yeah. Listen, John...what are you up to?"

"Nothing much. Just reading a little. Digesting Christmas dinner. Why?"

Katie didn't answer right away, her nerve failing.

Tower waited a moment, then asked, "You eat yet?"

"No," Katie admitted.

"Come over," Tower said. "I'll warm you something up."

"You sure?"

"I'm sure. You remember where I live?"

"Yeah. You had the unit barbeque there this summer."

"All right. Then I'll see you soon."

Katie nodded. "See you soon."

She hung up the phone and stared at it. Then she wiped away her tears, grabbed her jacket and left her desk behind.

Copyright ©2007 Frank Zafiro

The Christmas Tree Thief
Chris Grabenstein

On the most wonderful morning of the year, George Grimble marched across his snow-covered front lawn to screw a 60-watt light bulb inside the baby Jesus.

His family waited indoors, four noses pressed tight against the living room windows, and watched him weave his way across the most decorated five hundred square feet in the neighborhood. George gave them a jolly wave. They waved back, not quite as jollily. That was to be expected, he assumed. It was, after all, Christmas morning and his three young sons, still fully clad in their red-and-green holiday pajamas, were eager to tear into the piles of loot Santa had deposited underneath their tree. Visions of dancing sugarplums had been shoved aside by hopes for a new iPod.

That's why every year George Grimble insisted his children wait to open their presents until Jesus was fully illuminated in the outdoor nativity scene. He wanted to make certain his children remembered whose birthday was being celebrated this day. Sure, it was hard to keep the Christ in Christmas while every X-Box 360 sold was putting the X in Xmas, but that didn't mean he would simply surrender to the rampant over-commercialization of the holiday. No, sir. He'd do his gosh-darndest to keep alive the traditions established by his own parents: brass Advent angels spinning over three white and one red candle on the dining room table, a crèche scene set up in the family room, and a grand, brightly-illuminated, larger-than-life Nativity Scene in the front yard.

He heard a light tap on the window behind him. George turned around and saw Julia, his wife, giving him a spinning hand gesture that seemed to indicate he should hurry up and move things along. God bless her. It was 7 a.m. and she knew her children were eager to open their presents.

But not until Jesus was good-to-glow.

George moved a little faster through the decorations arrayed on his award-winning lawn.

They'd once again taken the top prize in the Homeowners Association's annual decorating contest. Thirteen thousand twinkle lights. Santa in his sleigh, pulled by eight not-so-tiny light-up reindeer. Rudolph's nose not only glowed, it blinked! Santa's Workshop inside an inflated snow globe. Plastic statues of twenty-four toy soldiers, thirty-six plastic choir boys, the Grinch (also inflatable and ten feet tall), Garfield in a Santa Hat, Frosty, Mickey and Minnie, a border of candy canes, various animated mechanical elves, and, this year's big addition—a snowman snowball fight sequence, sculpted out of rope lights and incorporating an independent microcontroller to create the animated illusion of two snowmen at opposite ends of the forty-foot-long flower bed hurling a snowball back and forth at each other.

All of it, of course, to highlight the main event in the center ring: the outdoor nativity scene. Six-foot-tall polyresin sculptures of Mary, Joseph, four shepherds (including the classic tall guy with the sheep slung over his shoulders), three sheep, one donkey, an ox, three wisemen, assorted angels, two camels (all that had come with the kit, even though it was historically inaccurate) and, of course, the baby Jesus, himself—swathed in angelic white diapers, his arms splayed out in eternal blessing, looking at least six months old, lying peacefully in his plastic wooden manger.

Yes, George could've screwed the light bulb up inside Jesus last night but that's not how his Dad used to do it. No sir. Christmas morning. First thing. The light of the world comes into the world at first light—dawn on Christmas day. Besides, the week old snow was crusted over with ice and that made finding all the extension cords, plugs, and outlets in the middle of the night somewhat difficult if not downright dangerous.

George knelt beside the plastic crib and realized he looked exactly like one of the hollow plastic shepherds only he wasn't holding out his hat in adoration of the Christ child. He was fumbling around inside the baby's shell, working his gloved hand down toward the small feet to find the light socket.

Funny. He remembered it being down near the feet.

No. Wait. That's Joseph and Mary. The baby's 60-watt bulb went up near the head—it made his halo glow brighter.

George scooted around on the snow. Twisted his arm and snagged his down coat on the rough edges of the baby's backside access hole. He had to slide sideways to get a better angle.

That's when he saw it.

The brand new Norway spruce down by the mailbox.

Somebody had lopped off its top!

George Grimble wrestled his arm out of the plastic Jesus and hurried down the curving, candy-cane lined path to the driveway. He heard tapping on the window again. Several sets of knuckles rapping on glass this time, probably the whole family, eager to tear into their presents.

Well, they'd just have to wait because some vandal had sawed off the perfectly pyramidical top to the spruce and left behind an ugly, two-foot-tall, stubby shrub. George could see sawdust flecked on the remaining limbs. Snapped branches. Ripped bark. Some hooligan was trying to ruin his holiday.

Fortunately, the tree near the mailbox hadn't been decorated– there were six "electronic trees" spread throughout the front yard. Strands of multi-colored lights cascading down from a central pole to create illuminated cones that were easier to set up and take down than twinkle lights wrapped around and around the real trees.

But, still—this was horrible! George had never felt so violated. He'd been vandalized in his own front yard.

He peeled off his glove and touched the jagged scar cut across the tree's sawed-off trunk. Still sticky. Still sappy. The wound was fresh.

The thief must've struck this morning! That meant he couldn't have gotten far. Unless he had a get-away vehicle. A car. Maybe a bike. This is why they needed a dog—to bark when criminals came prowling. George would have to talk to Julia about getting a dog again.

But not now. Now he had to find the Grinch who had attempted to steal his Christmas by cutting off the top to what was supposed to be his year-round Christmas tree, the evergreen serving as a constant reminder that, even in the middle of August, Christmas was coming!

***

"Can the boys open their presents now?" his wife asked.

George signaled for her to please be quiet. He was on the phone. "Please, honey—I'm talking to the police."

"But you're not saying anything."

"They put me on hold. Probably busy. Who knows where else this Christmas crook struck."

"Kyle accidentally tore open one of his presents." Julia said.

"We can fix that. Tape it shut."

"George? It's Christmas morning…."

"That doesn't mean felons get a free ride, dear. That's probably exactly what this juvenile delinquent was thinking: I can do anything I want on Christmas morning because the police will be too busy sipping eggnog-flavored coffee from Dunkin Donuts… yes, officer… no, sir… I was speaking to my wife. She was just brewing us up a pot."

George waved and pointed and gestured to Julia to start brewing coffee so the police couldn't arrest him for lying.

He then explained what happened.

"They sawed it off! Took the whole treetop. Ruined my entire landscape design. Well, I don't care. I want to press charges. Can't you dust the tree for prints? Well you should at least photograph the cut so you can do the forensics and match it to the saw blade this perpetrator probably keeps in the back of his pickup truck!"

Then the police officer explained how they were short staffed on account of the holiday and a minor traffic mishap out front of the Catholic Church where someone slowed down to look at the manger scene when the car behind them didn't.

"Well, when can you send someone out? What? You're just going to let them get away with this? I pay taxes, you know...."

The officer wished George a Merry Christmas.

Then he hung up on him.

"Please, George. The children need to open their presents. Now."

"We need a dog."

"Hunh?"

"To bark when thieves strike in the middle of the night."

"It's probably just some high school kids...."

George picked up his goose down coat. "Tell the children to wait."

"Wait?"

"They can't open their presents if I'm not there to shoot video."

"I could run the camera...."

"No, your job is to be Mrs. Claus and hand out the presents, one at a time...."

"We could do it differently this year...."

"Julia, please. I understand the children are eager to start their Christmas but I have to find out who did this to us or Christmas is ruined. Forever!"

"The tree will grow a new crown, George."

"Not in time for Christmas!"

"Well, maybe not this year, honey, but...."

"Hold on." George tromped into the living room. His three sons were sitting on the carpeted floor, glumly staring at the brightly wrapped mounds stacked beneath the twinkling boughs. "Morning, boys. Excuse me." He reached into the Mom pile and found the box he was looking for, shook it to make sure. "Boys?" he announced, "We're going to change things around a little this year. You'll eat your special, old-fashioned Christmas morning breakfast first, then we'll all open our presents a little later, after Daddy does a little detective work."

"What's that?" Sam, the middle child, pointed at the package George had in his hands.

George read the gift tag. "To Mrs. Claus from Mr. Claus. It's for your mom."

"She gets to open her presents now?" Sam whined.

"Just this one."

"That's not fair!"

"Samuel? Santa's still watching and remember: His return window is always open."

"Yes, sir."

Sam slunk back on his haunches and stared at the mountain of gifts he might never be allowed to open.

George went back to the kitchen where he smelled fresh coffee. Faintly egg-noggish. He held out the professionally wrapped package (the creases were so tight along the edges, they probably had some sort of wrapping machine at the catalog company) and presented it with a smile to Julia. "Here you go, hon. Merry Christmas!"

Julia sniffled back a tear. "What is it?"

"An Olde Fashioned Christmas Breakfast!"

"The box set from Swiss Colony?"

George nodded. "Yep! This year, it comes with Apple Cinnamon Pancake Mix, brown-sugar-cured ham, *and* Canadian-style bacon."

"So I'm supposed to cook breakfast while you traipse around the neighborhood looking for the top to your stupid tree?"

George knew she was angry at the situation, not him. "The catalog said it'd be 'a great start for Christmas morning' so why don't you guys go ahead and get started while I wrap up this other thing, okay?"

Julia didn't unwrap the box set. She didn't pour herself a reindeer mug full of fresh coffee. Instead, she stormed into the living room to most likely sit and sulk alongside her children.

Fine. George knew he was flying solo. He was like lawmen everywhere. An under-appreciated loner. One man standing against the darkness. But he wasn't in this for the thanks or the honor or the glory or even thrill of the chase.

He was in this for Justice.

***

First, George examined the physical evidence because that's what everybody always did on TV or in Sherlock Holmes stories.

He noted, once again, the sawdust flecking the clumps of branches directly beneath the cut. It probably drifted down while the perp sawed. He tried to memorize the tooth pattern of the saw blade and wondered if he should run inside and do a Google search on saw tooth dental patterns. Was this a Craftsman or a Wolfgarten brand blade? A handsaw or a chain saw? Most likely a handsaw—even if they didn't have a dog, somebody would've heard a chain saw screaming away near the mailbox first thing this morning.

To be absolutely certain, George hunkered down and checked the snow for oil residue. There was none, but he did notice something else: footprints! Boot prints! From size ten Chilkats Lace-Up Boots manufactured by The North Face.

The kind of boots George was wearing. He was looking at where he had just walked around the tree.

To be absolutely certain, he picked up his left foot and studied the tread pattern.

Yes. Just as he thought. He had been examining his own footprints in the snow.

And then he fell backwards. Hopping around on one foot in the snow had caused him to temporarily lose his balance.

"Merry Christmas, Mister Grimble!"

George looked up. It was Benny Bloomfeld—the eleven-year-old boy from across the street. He was whacking a hockey puck against the curb.

"Happy Chanukah, Benny."

"Chanukah's over. Two nights ago."

George nodded. "Of course." He always wondered why the Jewish people couldn't settle on a date for their holiday, why they had to keep moving it around. "That a new hockey stick?"

"Yes, sir. New puck, too. I also got some new ice skates but you can't really skate on asphalt too good, especially after they plow it."

George stood up. Dusted snow off his pants.

"Mr. Grimble?" Benny asked. "How come you're not inside opening presents with everybody else?" The young boy pointed. George turned around.

In the big living room window he saw Julia and his three sons, ripping wrapping paper off boxes, tossing tissue and ribbon up into the air. So. They had started without him and they weren't opening gifts in the proper order (youngest to oldest, one present each, then repeat).

"I'm investigating a crime," George explained to Benny Bloomfield.

"Really? Cool!"

At least Benny appreciated how George was spending his Christmas morning.

"Tell me, Benny—were you up early this morning?"

"Kind of. I guess. I wanted to practice my hockey."

"Did you happen to notice anything or anyone unusual?"

"Where?"

George pointed to the wounded spruce.

"Hey, somebody chopped off the top of your tree!"

George stared at Benny. In mystery books and in the movies, the criminal always returned to the scene of the crime. Was it purely coincidence that Benny had come out to play hockey against this particular curb this morning?

"Tell me, Benny—where were you this morning?"

"What time?"

"You tell me."

"I dunno. First, I was in bed, I guess. Then I went to the bathroom...."

"What kind of shoes are you wearing, Benny?"

"These? I dunno."

"Mind if I look at the treads?"

There were other footprints in the snow. One looked small enough to be Benny's.

"I need to go home, Mr. Grimble."

"Show me your shoes first, Benny."

He lunged at the boy's feet.

"Hey! Leave me alone!"

"Not until I see the treads on your Keds!"

That's when Benny Bloomfeld started

running.

George watched him flee across the street and peered at the soles of his shoes as he raced away but he boy was moving too fast to pick up a useable reading on the their tread pattern.

"Is everything okay out here, George?"

He turned around and saw Judy Green, the pretty blonde who lived next door. She was in her puffy white coat and unlaced snow boots.

"Someone vandalized my yard!" he explained.

"What'd they do?"

George shot her a look: *Isn't it obvious?*

After Mrs. Green shrugged, he pointed at the spruce.

"Ooh. Who does your pruning? Bartlett? Because we used them once and…."

"Some hoodlum did it this morning! They chopped off the top to my brand new evergreen tree!"

"Is that where you hide the speakers? In the tree?"

"Come again?"

"The speakers. For the Christmas carols every night."

"No. They're up by the porch."

Judy Green nodded. "We were wondering: Jim's folks are coming by later tonight for dinner and, well, I love 'Alvin and the Chipmunks' as much as anyone, but do you think maybe you could dial it down a notch this evening? Loud music makes Jim's dad jumpy. Something about the Korean War and hand grenades."

George gave her a sad nod. "To tell you the truth, Judy, I probably won't even turn the music on tonight. Doesn't feel much like Christmas. Not with this sort of person running around chopping down Christmas trees. I guess on Valentine's Day they go to graveyards to steal flowers...."

"Hey, you know what? Now that you mention it, this morning, when I was in the front room putting candy in the kids' stockings, I might've seen something...."

George perked up. This was it: the break he needed to crack the case.

"I thought it was kind of weird...."
"What was it?"
"It may not be anything...."
"Let me be the judge of that, Mrs. Green. Please—tell me what you saw!"
"Well, it was dark. All your lights weren't lit...."
"They're on a timer."
She nodded. "It was a silhouette. Somebody short."
"A kid?"
"Maybe. Like I said, it was only a silhouette, so I didn't see any detail but whoever he was, he was dragging a spindly little tree behind him in the snow." She laughed. "Reminded me of that Charlie Brown Christmas special on TV, you know the one I

mean?"

George knew. He tilted his head toward the plastic Peanuts gang set up near the plastic Santa-with-his-list. Charlie Brown, Linus, Lucy, Schroeder, Snoopy—the whole gang, their mouths in perfect cartoon circles as they harmonized around a scrawny tree.

"Yeah," said Mrs. Green. "The shadow guy had a real Charlie Brown Christmas Tree."

Or the top to George Grimble's Norway spruce.

"Which way did he go?"

She pointed left. "Up the street

"Thank you, Mrs. Green. Do you remember anything else?"

"No. Not really. Except…."

"Except what?"

"For a split second, I remember seeing his feet."

"And?"

"I think he was wearing slippers. Bedroom slippers."

***

He was.

There was a trail of small, flat footprints, right near the edge of the curb. The kind you could only make with slippers or maybe moccasins.

Snow made it so easy to track a criminal. It was like an instant plaster cast, this thing they did on all the CSI shows when some perpetrator was sloppy enough to step in the mud under a window.

His head tilted down and his eyes fixed on the ground, George Grimble was on the right path to save Christmas. He knew this was about more than apprehending the individual who had defiled his tree. This depraved villain had undoubtedly cut off the head of the spruce to send a sick message to the world: don't you dare celebrate your holiday in public. The mad ax man was most likely a radical member of that whole politically-correct bunch but this creep was too big a chicken to risk electrocution going after the big displays: Santa's workshop, the snowball-tossing snowmen, even (may God have mercy on his twisted soul) the Nativity Scene. So the coward took out his cheap little handsaw and hacked away at the easiest target he could find: the innocent little tree.

The trail of slipper-prints led down the slight hill and to the left, to the older part of the neighborhood, the section with brick split levels left over from the 70s. The last hefty house was on George's right. It ruled its lot like George's stout little mansion ruled his. The folks over in this area only had two bathrooms, tops, and usually gave out miniature candy bars to the kids on Halloween instead of the real deals.

Now George saw needles. Green spruce needles. A half-crushed cone.

The poor tree had been manhandled.

The slipper prints left the street and

headed up over the curb and onto a concrete pathway that led to a short stoop of brick steps and an unadorned front door.

    58 Eggert Avenue.

    Gotcha!

    George surveyed the premises. No Christmas or Chanukah or Kwanzaa or even Ramadan decorations. Nothing to indicate the holidays had even come to this corner of the suburbs. George had been right. Christmas-haters lived here. Instead of building up their own holiday traditions, whatever faith they might follow, they had decided to tear down somebody else's. His.

    Well, they weren't going to get away with it, not on George Grimble's watch.

    He pressed the doorbell. Heard it ring. Pressed it again. Harder.

    He was ready to pound on the door when, finally, it swung open.

    A short, frail man in a bathrobe and slippers stood in the darkness on the other side.

    The slippers were wet.

    "Merry Christmas," the old man said.

    George huffed out an exasperated, "Ha!"

    "May I help you?"

    George was craning his neck, trying to see behind the ancient little gnome because he heard a strange clicking noise from somewhere inside the house. Click, click, click. The noise came in rhythmic beats. He also smelled sour soup. Chicken noodle.

"Have we met?" the old man asked, his voice thin and reedy.

"No," said George. "I don't think we have. I'm George Grimble. I live around the corner and up the block at 42 Merry Dell Road."

"The house with all the decorations!" the man said, sounding like a kid who's just met the real Santa Claus for the first time at his castle in the mall.

"That's right," said George coldly.

"Such a beautiful display!"

"It used to be."

"Oh, dear. What happened?"

"Well, sir," George said sarcastically, because this whole wide-eyed-delight act wasn't working on him, "It seems we were vandalized earlier this morning."

George's eyes finally adjusted to the darkness filling the room on the far side of the door and he saw it, sitting in the middle of a cluttered coffee table—the top to his Norway spruce. "Seems somebody chopped off the head of my favorite tree!"

The elderly man dropped his eyes.

"That, sir," he said, sounding ashamed, "was me."

Good. A confession. George wouldn't have to dust for prints or run a polygraph or check the dental work on the old man's saw.

The thief reached into the pocket of his baggy robe. "I had to use my Swiss army knife to cut her down. Has a little saw blade in here. Thought I could snap it off with my hands but I couldn't...."

"Just a minute, sir—anything you say can and will be used against you in a court of law!"

"I know. I'm sorry. I was out so early, five a.m.; I didn't want to wake you to ask permission. And seeing how you had all those other wonderful decorations, I figured you wouldn't miss a foot or two off the top...."

"Well, sir—you figured wrong!"

"Charlie?" a weak voice called from somewhere at the edge of the darkness. "Who's at the door?"

The old man gestured for George to come into his home. George did so, but only after the bandit closed up his nasty-looking knife blade.

"Dorothy, this is our neighbor...from up the hill. I'm sorry I don't know your name...."

George was too furious to look at whoever this Dorothy might be. He was staring at his wilting treetop, propped up inside a rusty coffee can half-filled with water. Someone had draped it with a string of popcorn and topped it with a wad of aluminum foil, crumpled so it vaguely resembled a star.

"My name is George," he stammered. "George Grimble. And that, right there, used to be the top to my brand new Norway spruce!"

"Bless you," said the weak voice.

George heard that click-click-click again. He swung his eyes over toward the annoying noise and saw the old man standing behind a withered woman slumped sideways in a wheelchair far too big for her shrunken body. She had a plastic tube inserted in her nostrils. The tube snaked down to a green canister on wheels. Oxygen. A regulator pump.

Click-click-click.

"I didn't know where Charlie was going to find a Christmas tree when I woke up and told him I had changed my mind: that I didn't want to spend my last Christmas without a tree…."

The old man brushed her snowy white hair away from her rheumy eyes. "Now, Dorothy, the doctor never said this would be your last…."

"He didn't have to." She smiled gently at George. "You don't smoke, do you?"

"No, ma'am."

"Good. Don't start. Mr. Grimble, I simply can't thank you enough for giving us our last-minute Christmas tree." She halted. Waited for more oxygen to reach her weary lungs. "Ever since the doctors gave us their grim report, I'm afraid I've been something of a grouch." Another gasp for breath. "Poor Charlie. I told him: I don't want any decorations this year, none at all…."

"'Not even a tree' she told me." The old man named Charlie sounded like he might weep.

"I didn't want to be reminded of all those Christmases come and gone knowing I'll never see one again." To George's surprise, the woman smiled. "Well, Mr. Grimble, this morning I changed my mind."

"Always a woman's prerogative," said Charlie with a conspiratorial wink to George.

"Oh, I made quite a scene. Sobbing in my pillow, wishing we had a Christmas tree. Nothing fancy. Just something green and fragrant." She pointed at the small pyramid of spruce limbs topped with a wad of aluminum foil. "In all my eighty-six Christmases, I swear I don't think I've ever laid eyes on a finer tree. Bless you, Mr. Grimble."

George wanted to say something but could only nod.

"Of course, I didn't ask for all the fancy decorations," Dorothy said, pointing at the popcorn garlands and homemade star.

"Well, dear," said Charlie, "every Christmas tree needs a star up top. It's a tradition. Isn't that right, Mr. Grimble?"

George felt a lump in his throat. "Yes, sir. It is. Well, uh—Merry Christmas, ma'am. I think I better head home. My children are eager to open their presents."

"Tell them I already opened mine!" She beamed at the scrawny tree that really wasn't a tree, just the top of a Norway spruce planted for what Real Estate agents called "curb appeal."

Charlie walked George toward the door.

"How much do I owe you?" Charlie whispered when they were outside on the stoop. "To replace the tree?" He reached into his robe, found his wallet.

"Nothing."

"You sure?"

George nodded.

And then he asked his neighbor if his wife might enjoy a traditional Christmas morning breakfast of Apple Cinnamon Pancakes served with brown-sugar-cured ham *and* Canadian-style bacon. When they said "yes," he asked them to wait while he ran home to grab his car so he could give them a ride around the corner and up the block.

As he made his way back up the candy-cane lined path to tell his family of the invited guests, George noticed the light glowing inside the baby Jesus. Funny. He didn't remember having screwed the bulb in.

Copyright ©2007 Chris Grabenstein

A Piece of Christmas
Deborah Elliott-Upton

Arlen pinched a bit of snuff between his thumb and forefinger and stuffed it between his lip and gums. As saliva mixed with the ground tobacco leaves, his gums tingled for a few seconds, then the feeling subsided. Footsteps on the brick walkway behind him startled him. His right eye twitched. Arlen didn't like surprises. The Cunninghams were finally home for the evening and signaled his shift's end. Another Saturday night dead and gone and Arlen's wallet richer, but his soul depleted as much as if he'd sliced off a piece of it to sell to Lucifer himself.

In fact, he *had* sold his soul to the devil, but that was over two years ago and something he tried to forget. Arlen repented and had made vows to a new wife, Shelly, since then. He figured his slate was clean with the Big Guy.

He'd lost more than Hallie, the sweet-eyed girl he'd known only five days before she introduced him to a world of betrayal. In the outcome, he'd lost his first wife, twenty-two years on the job, and a sweet pension just a few years down the road. Now he worked freelance security jobs for rich people who were always traveling somewhere. To the south of France when the weather turned chilly or to Monaco for a little gambling or to

Rio for cocktails with friends.

Arlen tipped his hat to Mrs. Cunningham, a good quarter century younger than her husband. Spoiled rotten, Arlen thought as he watched her skinny behind sashay into the house. She dripped with diamonds that could choke the chihuahua carried in her purse like a gaudy, unneeded scarf.

Mr. Cunningham, with his disheveled hair and thick, black horn-rimmed glasses, dug into his pocket and removed a gold money clip. He counted crisp one hundred dollar bills and held them out for Arlen. He always paid in cash, which was good enough as far as Arlen was concerned, but it irritated him Cunningham made him take the money instead of handing it to him. He always did that. In fact, he'd never shaken Cunningham's hand. Probably thought he was too good for that. Arlen reached for the money and although he wanted to snatch it from Cunningham, he didn't. He carefully took the money and stabbed it into his front trouser pocket.

As Arlen bent to spit the tobacco juice toward the topiary, Cunningham held up a hand in a stopping motion. "Don't," he said. "You know Mrs. Cunningham doesn't like that."

"Sorry, sir," Arlen said. "I forgot." The spit lodged against his tongue. He held back a gag.

"A nasty habit," Cunningham said. "You really should quit."

"Yes, sir," Arlen said, mentally spitting on Cunningham's well-shined Italian leather shoes.

"Oh, and Matthews," Cunningham said. "We'll need you all of next week."

"Leaving again so soon, Mr. Cunningham?" Tobacco juice inched along his tongue, threatening to slide down the back of his throat. "Where to now?"

"No, no," Cunningham said. "We'll be home for the holidays. It's just that we'll need more security. Since it's Christmas and all."

"Of course, sir." Cunningham was one of those who expected a "sir" attached to practically every sentence. Arlen had met his type repeatedly through his years on the force. Always someone higher on the economic scale to look down on him and demand what should have been given out of respect. Money has its privilege all right.

"Just so many parties and of course, we'll need extra security on Thursday."

Actually, the Cunninghams didn't *need* extra security at all. Arlen *was* the extra security. With the system they had, Arlen was simply paid to be seen. The Cunninghams thought it deterred crime more than a sign announcing they owned a security system. In fact, they liked showing off they could afford the extra and unnecessary help.

"Thursday, sir?"

"We're hosting a gala on Christmas Eve."

A gala? What kind of guy says *hosting a gala*? "Yes, sir," Arlen said.

Evan Cunningham shivered. "We'll talk about it tomorrow. It's beginning to sleet, isn't it?"

Before Arlen could answer, Cunningham turned and headed into the house.

Dismissed, Arlen thought. *Damn rich bastard dismissed me like I was a servant.* Arlen spat the tobacco juice on the grass and watched for a moment as the sleet turning to ice clustered on top of the spittle, hiding it from view.

Working Christmas Eve and probably Christmas Day, too. The wife wasn't gonna like it, but maybe she'd like the extra shopping money for the day after Christmas sales. He would stress that fact with Shelly. After the holidays, Arlen would be hard-pressed to find as much work, so he had to jump on every opportunity now.

As Arlen reached his SUV, his stomach growled. He bent over and spat a big wad of dark tobacco juice on the Cunningham's curb. *Just marking my territory*, he thought. He climbed into the Explorer and for some reason he didn't understand, started laughing. Starting the engine, the old baby roared to life on the third try. Beneath the rumbling, the vehicle shuddered like a wet dog throwing off the falling sleet. Arlen continued laughing and didn't stop until the Cunningham mansion was only a memory in the rearview mirror.

The week before Christmas was a flurry of the Cunninghams either departing from and arriving to their home and out again like they were in a strange rat race no one could see. Arlen imagined the Cunninghams on a giant hamster wheel running at top speed and never making any headway, but never stopping to ask why.

The Cunninghams arrived with boxes and parcels to be brought into the house like clockwork and for some reason, they thought that was part of the security job for which they'd hired Arlen.

Carting in yet another bag from Delancey's with more paper stuffed inside than substance, Arlen's curiosity got the best of him. Delancey's was the premiere shop for the Yuppies of the new Millennium, or whatever was the proper term these days. Arlen didn't much care. They were all Rich Old Bastards to him. The R.O.B.'s kept the economy alive and that was about it, he decided. Not good for much else except keeping poor slobs like him in a weekly paycheck grind.

Arlen's mouth filled with tobacco juice and he wiped a hand across his mouth to hold the spittle back. He hurried through the kitchen door and laid the packages on the counter, searching for the trash bin. He spat on top of garbage, watching the brown liquid seep down into the trash liner. An outer lettuce leaf was to the side. Arlen yanked the lettuce over the top to hide the tobacco juice.

He returned to the bags, glancing around to see no one was within eyesight. He pried back the stiff white tissue papers with the gilt edging peeping from the tops of the pale pink linen store bags. At the bottom of the bag was a tiny box, the kind housing diamond bracelets. Of course, Arlen only knew that from the movies and those jewelry store commercials that contaminated the airways before every Christmas, Valentine's Day and Mother's Day. Damn things made it hard to be a regular guy who couldn't give his sweetie anything remotely like that, so he looked like a sap to his girl and made her envious of those that could. Shelly definitely envied Mrs. Cunningham's lifestyle.

Working for the Cunninghams did have its moments. Last year Mrs. Cunningham personally left Arlen an envelope on Christmas Eve. Inside was a thousand bucks.

So easy to be generous when you don't have to ask how much or wait for a payday to buy your lady dinner out.

"A piece of Christmas for you, Arlen," she'd said like she was giving her doggie a treat.

Arlen had shared the bonus with his wife. Sort of. Five hundred dollars was enough to make Shelly happy. *It doesn't hurt a man to have a secret stash of his own*, Arlen thought. So, he tucked away half a grand into a safety deposit box he'd had back when he was running with Hallie. One of those ***Open 24/7*** places, the safety deposit box had been opened with an alias that only he knew about. Safer than Ft. Knox. Only two things occupied the box now; his half of the bonus and the 9 mm. he'd taken from the body of Carlos Molina two years ago. It never hurt to carry extra insurance.

Arlen considered taking the bracelet box, one they'd probably never miss and present it to his woman this Christmas instead of the replacement toaster oven she'd requested. Just once he wanted to show Shelly she meant something more than a security guard's wife. *Just once*, he thought. But, he didn't dare. Not after what happened with Hallie.

Arlen slipped upstairs to the guestroom and deposited the bags along with the others decorating the carpeting like fallen rose petals on a bride's wedding day. Pristine, the pink bags stood like sentinels on the white carpeting. Standing at attention waiting for the plum fairy to scoop them up and distribute them to her friends who needed another diamond like he needed another debt.

He cursed under his breath at the senselessness of it all, the rich getting richer and the poor getting more of the same old, same old this Christmas. Why did success drip on some and become a downpour on others?

Evan Cunningham had inherited his money and his wife had married into it. Arlen and Shelly would never wallow in money. They'd be lucky to wade up to their pinkie toe. A piece of Christmas would be the closest they'd ever get to the big time.

The packages delivered, Arlen headed back outside to patrol the grounds. He varied his route and time just in case someone paid attention. The last thing he needed was a robbery to take place during his watch.

Evan Cunningham stepped out onto the front walkway. "Hold up, Matthews," he said.

"Yes, sir." Arlen crossed the lawn to stand within six feet of his employer.

"We'll be out the rest of the evening. Probably not home until late. I'd like you to stay until we return."

"Yes, sir." Arlen fingered the stun gun, almost wishing he had a chance to use it. For the year and a half he'd worked for the Cunningham's, he'd only drawn his gun once and that was when a squirrel pirouetted from a tree when a neighborhood cat scared it.

Mrs. Cunningham appeared at the front door. A tall woman, she wore a black sable that hit the back of her knee. The coat would fall closer to full length on Shelly and would have swallowed Hallie.

The Cunningham's Porsche edged out of the garage slowly. *A shame,* Arlen thought. *That car should be driven, not inched along the roadway.*

He watched the car disappear down the street, its right blinker a red flash reminding Arlen of Rudolph. Hallie had a thing for Rudolph, he remembered and chuckled softly.

As he trailed through the rose garden and around the pool house, Arlen wondered if the Cunninghams even knew how much they were worth. Would their quality of life be interrupted if they were robbed?

A movement caught Arlen's attention and the hairs on the back of his neck—a human version of antennae—stood on end. Arlen remembered the excitement of rushing to a robbery in progress. His heartbeat quickened and his right hand snaked to his holster and released the catch. The Glock 19 felt good in his hand, like an appendage he'd almost forgotten.

He moved stealthily through the rose bushes, his heels grazing the ground. Arlen ducked down and kept still for a moment and listened. A sudden wind tripped through the naked tree branches like a harpist barely touching strings. Then it was quiet. Too quiet. Eerily quiet.

What the hell's happened to the security system? Arlen wondered.

A snap of twig beneath a footstep crackled in the air like the first firecracker on the fourth of July. Arlen's head jerked to the sound's source. Sudden movement of a man dressed in a black head to toe and a stocking mask pulled over his face left little chance of this being anything but a robbery in progress.

Arlen stood, his hands stretched out in front of him in an inverted V with the Glock like a witch finder. He was about to shout for the thief to stop, when he lowered his gun.

The robber had removed the mask and repositioned it, then slid it back against his face. *He was incredibly young, but weren't they all?* he thought. Young and impatient. Impatient for the good things in life that seemed to come to people like the Cunninghams and never to those that deemed robbery their only answer. Maybe he was like Hallie or maybe he was like Arlen was back then, wanting nothing more than providing his lover with a gift she deserved. Only Hallie hadn't gotten what she deserved and Arlen was to blame.

His decision had ultimately been to take her down along with the gang she ran with— the ones who sent her to take an older cop as a lover and persuade him to look the other way. His obsession for her led to the breakup of his marriage, the end of his police career and Hallie being incarcerated for 10 years, a chance of serving only seven with good behavior. He doubted the waif-like Hallie would survive even half her sentence.

He might have allowed her to get away with the robbery if she hadn't betrayed him with Carlos Molina. Arlen's revenge cost Carlos his life, Hallie her freedom and Arlen everything else.

The would-be robber crouched down beneath the library windows of the Cunningham estate. He made his way to the French doors, staying in the shadows for the most part.

Arlen knew he should stop the kid before he got inside. A good lawyer could cite trespassing instead of a breaking and entering charge if Arlen stopped him now.

Yes, he should step forward now. *Take the kid now*, he thought. But, he didn't. He watched, almost like this was a movie playing out before him. An interactive movie where he was involved, only from a distance and without danger. He kept wondering how the kid managed to get past the security system. The Cunninghams had paid top dollar for state-of-the-art. Arlen tried to remember if he'd seen the kid's face before tonight. Perhaps he worked for the security system provider. He shook his head. He couldn't be sure. They were all young pups and he'd not cared about how the system worked as long as it worked.

The robber worked on the lock and opened it in record time. Arlen was impressed, but not surprised. Like any occupation, thieves practiced their trade, honing their skills until they could do it blindfolded. The kid darted into the house. Arlen advanced to the house, crossing the distance quickly. Inside, the robber stood near the doorway for a few seconds. When he moved down the hallway to the left, Arlen followed. The kid knew the floorplan. Good, he'd studied first. Maybe he did have an inside view when the system was installed.

The kid then crept up the back stairs, taking the steps two at a time. At the landing, he half-turned then continued up. Arlen followed him to the top of the stairs, his Glock leading the way.

He should stop him now. Now, before only the kid's Christmas holidays would be ruined instead of looking at a long jail term, maybe he'd get probation. If Arlen stopped him now… but he didn't.

The kid ducked inside the Cunningham bedroom suite. Arlen wondered where he'd gotten his information on the floorplan. So far, he hadn't made a mistake. Except for not knowing the Cunninghams hired an extra security patrolman for the nights they were away from the house. How had he missed that? The kid was a rookie, all right and that one mistake would cost big.

Arlen watched the kid go to the bed and strip off the covers. He yanked a pillow off the bed and separated the case from the pillow. He headed directly for the closet. Opening the door, the automatic light flooded the room, spilling out over the white carpeting like newly-fallen snow. Wasting no time, the robber found the jewelry box hidden in the walk-in closet's wall. He pried the lock with a simple twist and began unloading its contents into the pillow case.

Arlen stared at the kid, seeing his impulsiveness by scraping the shelves with one swipe. Several brooches fell to the white carpeted floor, but the kid was in a hurry.

Why are you doing this kid?

Arlen needed a pinch of snuff. Bad. *I should take the kid now*, he thought. But he didn't.

The kid moved quickly, his foot barely missing the half dozen brooches. He made a final swipe, then closed the pillowcase in a crude knot. He slung the sack over his back and dressed all in black, reminded Arlen of a Bizarro-world Santa, taking instead of giving. Dark and angry instead of happy and bright.

Arlen inched back into the hallway, hiding in yet another bedroom no one occupied. The kid stormed down the hallway and to the stairs without a glance back.

Arlen should stop him now. Now while he was still inside the house. Now while he still had the air of imprudence upon him of getting away. Now while Arlen still could claim to be doing his job.

But, he didn't.

Instead, he dogged the kid's steps through the house, leaving as he'd entered. Arlen thought about the kid's future being swallowed up in a long line of burglaries, each take never enough to last. Arlen sighed. He couldn't do it. Someone had to stop the kid from ruining his life.

Two steps to the kid's one, Arlen crept up behind him. Breathing hard from the sudden exertion, Arlen's whoosh of breath raised hairs on the kid's neck The kid started to turn, but his reaction too late. Arlen raised the stun gun to the kid's neck and pressed the switch. The kid crumpled like a paper napkin and fell to the floor just as noiselessly.

Arlen fought to catch his breath. Adrenalin coursed through him like no high he'd ever felt before. He'd missed the chase, the collar, the pure splendor of an honest takedown in action. Damn, it was good to feel alive again.

He snapped handcuffs on the kid's wrists. With twine from the butler's pantry, he tied the would-be burglar like he had in his calf-roping days just because he still remembered how, and secured him to the massive wooden *armoire*. The kid wasn't going anywhere. Chances were he wouldn't call for help, but Arlen gagged him with one of the Cunningham's Irish linen napkins.

Arlen stepped outside the library's French doors and watched his breath materialize, then disappear before him. The sleet had turned into snow and fell daintily on the silent night. He stepped back inside, feeling the sudden gush of warmth as the heater kicked on in response to the cold blast creeping through the library's open doors.

Arlen imagined calling the precinct,

hearing the soft cheers of his fellow officers as he brought in the Christmas-time thief. It wouldn't be like that, he knew. He'd burned his bridges and taken a shortcut to hell.

His mind reeled with visions of the haughty Cunninghams being interviewed by their insurance broker and not being half as overwrought as the young man had been when Arlen glimpsed his peach-fuzzed face in the garden.

Arlen trudged upstairs to the master bedroom and scooped up the fallen and forgotten brooches. He carried them to the guest bedroom where he dumped them ceremoniously into the bag where he'd spotted the diamond bracelet box. It was easy to find as his snuff-spittled hands had grazed the top of the white tissue paper, marking it as easily as if he'd written his name across Delancey's on the bag. He plucked the gift bags one by one, emptying their contents into the one he'd marred.

He tossed the gift bags behind him like a snow blower with pink paper and white tissues billowing across the room like confetti on New Year's Eve. Except the one gift bag with the tobacco stain that he placed inside the Explorer. Arlen started up the vehicle and let the engine idle for a few minutes until the heater kicked in. He warmed his hands against the heater vent, then shifted into drive.

He returned to the Cunningham estate in less than twelve minutes. That's when he made the call to the police stating there had been a robbery at the mansion with one thief tied-up in the living room and another who'd gotten away with at minimum the Cunningham's jewelry.

The kid would do a stretch, probably less time than he deserved. He'd been too good for this to be his first job. Even if he didn't realize it, Arlen provided the kid an opportunity. He'd have to make the choice for himself. Perhaps getting caught would deter his life of crime, he thought, then laughed. *Only happens that way in the movies.*

The detectives would question the kid, demanding to know the identity of his accomplice and where they could find the jewelry. Arlen smiled thinking of the kid steadfastly arguing he'd done the crime alone. *Who'd believe him?*

Yes, a good chance of him losing his job existed, but he would be losing that in a few days anyway. The thought of Carlos' gun and half his Christmas bonus having company for a while made him smile.

Arlen pulled a pinch of snuff from the packet and shoved it next to his gums. The tingle sent a shiver down to his toes. By the time the Cunninghams arrived, he needed to spit. He walked over to the topiary and grinned. It was going to be a good Christmas after all. Tonight he'd been given a real piece of Christmas, all shiny and bright and wrapped up beneath the tree.

Copyright ©2007 Deborah Elliott-Upton

Santa Solves A Murder
Jan Christensen

Just as the young boy sat down in his lap, Santa pushed him off, dashed down the three stairs that led to his throne-like chair and chased Jimmy MacIntyre toward the mall's north exit. Behind him, he heard someone say, "Is Santa drunk again?" And someone else answered, "Looks like the devil's after him."

No, he was after Jimmy Mac. The same Jimmy Mac who disappeared three days ago and whose wife had hired Santa to find him.

Of course, when Mrs. Mac hired Santa, she didn't know that he moonlighted from his P.I. business to play Santa in the mall every year. *Ho, ho, ho,* he thought as he avoided a kid zipping down the floor in some of those new sneakers with the wheels imbedded in the back and nearly collided with a woman pushing a stroller.

"Go, Santa, go!" someone shouted.

He felt his padded stomach shift downwards, getting in the way of his legs. Jimmy Mac hadn't yet realized that Santa was gaining on him, but it could happen any moment.

Unless Santa ran into the display of books in front of the bookstore, which he almost did. Or tripped over a teenage window-shopper oblivious to the on-coming Santa. Santa fell on his unpadded backside and slid a few yards across the fake marble floor. Wig askew, he flew to his feet and looked to see where Jimmy Mac had gone.

And couldn't find him. Rubbing his sore butt, he limped down the floor, looking in the shops for a sign of Jimmy, but didn't see him. At the exit, he went outside and looked around.

No Jimmy Mac.

Sighing, Santa went back to Santa's Corner to find the mall manager standing there, hands on hips and scowling. "Where the hell did you go?" she asked.

"Don't swear in front of the kiddies," Santa said and climbed back onto his throne. He really needed to lose about forty pounds.

"I'm sure they've heard worse," Ingrid Scruggs said. "Fix your wig. You can't just leave like that."

"I just did," Santa said, adjusting the fake hair on his almost bald head. A little boy stared at him solemnly, thumb in mouth. Santa smiled at him. "Saw an old friend—hadn't seem him in years. I was trying to catch up with him, but he got away."

"Santa's funny," said a small voice.

"Yeah," said another. "I like this Santa better than the other one. He smelled funny."

"That was liquor," said the first voice.

Ingrid stared at the speakers with an appalled look on her face.

"Jerry drinks?" she whispered to Santa.

"Afraid so," Santa said. "But he's nice to the kids."

"Well, please don't go running off

again," Ingrid said faintly. "It makes the parents nervous."

"Right." He gestured for a little girl to come sit in his lap and whisper in his ear what she wanted for Christmas. Giggling, she did so, and Ingrid went away, probably to chew someone else out.

During a lull, Ginny, cute in an elf's outfit, asked Santa about why he'd run off.

Santa explained and pulled a picture of Jimmy Mac out of his pocket. "If you see him, let me know, okay? I really need to find him. His wife is worried. At least I can tell her he seems to be okay." Santa adjusted his padded stomach and motioned for a mother to put her screaming little boy in his lap. "There, there," he soothed. "I'm one of the good guys."

Yeah, a regular knight in shining armor. Or rather, a Santa in a red suit. As the boy continued to scream, Ginny tried to get a decent picture. Finally the mother took him back, looking embarrassed, and walked away without a word.

Mrs. Jimmy MacIntyre was a gorgeous woman, the type who was in every P.I. novel and every man's dreams, especially for what many would consider an "older woman." She was about forty, he figured. She came into his office in a cloud of perfume and wearing a suit of some yellow nubby material with black trim. The skirt didn't quite reach her perfect knees, and the legs showing were incredible. Black spike heels emphasized her calves and the shape of her feet. She had high, firm breasts and a nice face—not movie-star beautiful, but pleasant. Diamond ring, large but tasteful, on her wedding ring finger, pearl choker and bracelet completed her outfit. She smiled at P. I. Phil High and sat down, tugging on her skirt.

"Can you find someone for me?" she purred.

"Sure," Phil said, trying not to gasp, gulp, stare or otherwise embarrass himself.

Her smile dazzled. "Great." Then she sobered. "I haven't seen my husband for three days. He went off to work in the morning and never came home."

"What's he do for a living?" P. I. Phil asked.

"He's an insurance agent. Homes, cars."

"I see," Phil said, wondering if the pearls were real, the suit a knockoff. How much did insurance agents make, anyway? "Has he ever disappeared before?"

"No, never. I talked to the police, but they didn't seem very concerned.

Phil tried to look concerned. "That's just their cop demeanor," he said. "I'm sure they're trying to find him."

"In their spare time," she scoffed. "I figure if I hire you, it won't be something you do when you have the time. You'd devote all your energy to it, right?"

"Of course," P. I. Phil said, biting his tongue so he wouldn't tell her about Santa.

"You have a photo?"

She dug into her purse and handed him one.

He looked down at it. Jimmy Mac was an average-looking guy except for the scar running from the outer edge of his left eyebrow down to his jaw. "Um, how'd he get that scar?" Phil asked. It would be hard for Jimmy to hide.

Mrs. MacIntyre shrugged. "He won't talk about it. I think it happened in his wild youth. Maybe even a gang or something." She gave a slight shiver and smiled at him.

Strange reaction, Phil thought. Wondering if the scar had anything to do with his disappearance, he asked the wife for address and phone number, more details about Jimmy Mac, settled on a fee, and saw her out the door.

For three days, when not playing Santa, Phil had been looking for Jimmy Mac. And he came up totally empty. What a coincidence to see him in the mall today. Actually, how strange that Jimmy Mac was wandering around in the mall, if he wanted to hide from his wife. What if she'd been shopping?

On his break, Phil called Mrs. Mac's number on his cell. No answer.

When he walked back to Santa's Corner, he saw another Santa sitting on the throne. The whole mall appeared deserted, and no one was waiting to talk to Santa. Ginny wasn't back from her break, either. When he came closer, he saw that it was Larry in the seat, asleep—probably drunk. Surprised since Larry wasn't due to take over for another two hours, Phil shook him on the shoulder, but Larry's head lolled to one side, and Phil could see something red oozing from under his white beard. Blood.

Phil took a step backwards and almost fell off the tiny platform. He stumbled down the steps and bumped into Ginny.

"What's Larry doing here so early?" Ginny asked.

"Good question." Phil flipped open his phone and dialed 9-1-1. "I'm at Treetop Mall, and there's a dead Santa in Santa's Corner. You need to come pick him up. No, lady, I'm not kidding." He hung up and stared at Larry.

Ginny tugged his sleeve. "He's dead? How?"

"Dunno."

"How do you know he's dead, then?"

"He looks dead."

"Drunk, maybe."

"No. He's not breathing, Ginny."

Ginny sank down on the bottom step to the throne and put her head in her hands.

Phil stood and thought. Another coincidence. The day abounded in them. Phil shifted his Santa's padding and tried Mrs. Mac's number again. Again, no answer.

"You'd better call Ingrid," Ginny said, her voice muffled by her hands still covering her face. "She's gonna be mad."

"That'll put her in a good mood," Phil said. "She likes being mad." He found the Mall's main number in his phone. When Ingrid answered he told her to get down to Santa's Corner as fast as she could. He hung up on her sputtering.

The police arrived, and chaos ensued. They set up a tent-like structure around Larry so the crowd couldn't see what was going on. Ingrid arrived and was afraid they'd shut down the whole mall, but they only cordoned off Santa's Corner. They asked Phil and Ginny and Ingrid to stick around. They kept the crowd back, but many lingered, especially angry parents who had come to have their children's pictures taken with Santa.

A tug on his arm made Phil turn. Mrs. Mac whispered, "Any news about Jimmy?" She looked around nervously.

"I saw him earlier, here in the mall." Why wasn't she surprised to see him in a Santa suit?

"Oh!"

"I was surprised. I mean, what if you'd been here and seen him, too?"

She shrugged. "I go to the gym every morning—just came from there."

"And you just happened to see me here now."

She avoided his eyes. "Yes."

"You're lying." His voice rose a bit, and they both looked around. The only one seeming to pay any attention was Ginny. Her expression was impossible for Phil to read. Certainly not her usual innocent, perky self.

Phil lowered his voice. "I think you knew all along I worked as a Santa here." He took her arm and led her farther away from the crowd. "What's the real story?"

Mrs. Mac began to tremble. She hugged herself and shook so hard that Phil looked around for somewhere they could sit down.

He led her to a bench, and she sank into it as if dissolving.

"Tell me," Phil said, impatient with his heavy Santa suit and the padding which got in the way of his sitting closer to her.

Mrs. Mac looked up at him, eyes brimming with unshed tears. "I think Jimmy killed La . . . that man. The other Santa."

"Larry," Phil said. "You knew Larry."

Mrs. Mac shook her head violently. "No. No. I don't know anything. I just know Jimmy disappeared, and I need to find him."

Phil shook *his* head. "There are too many coincidences here, Mrs. MacIntyre. You hire me three days ago, I see your husband today, Larry is murdered today, and you show up right afterwards."

"I just came to do some shopping and saw the commotion," she said weakly.

"Look, I can't help you if you don't come clean with me," Phil said. He was getting impatient, but he knew that wouldn't help. He looked around and saw Ginny had moved, too. She was standing pretty close, but he didn't think she could hear them. Was she involved? Cute, innocent-looking Ginny?

He began to think of the possibilities. Something to do with the kids coming to see Santa. He refused to think the worst—about kids and predatory adults. Mrs. Mac just didn't seem the type to be involved in anything so horrific.

So, what type was she? Obviously, she liked the things money could buy. Perhaps she didn't have a very strong moral sense. Maybe she'd go as far as larceny, but not murder.

What scam could be pulled here? Larry's ghost seemed to whisper something in Phil's ear. Something Charles Dickensian about pickpockets. Could it be as simple as that? A gang of pickpockets? But how could that lead to murder? Certainly, picking pockets only earned a few months in jail for the first offense, not the years and years that murder could bring. And nothing in his background checks of Mrs. and Mrs. MacIntyre had indicated either had spent any time in jail previously.

He tried to remember if he'd seen either of them before while working, but he couldn't recall. He was always so focused on the kids. And they probably wore scarves and heavy coats to hide their appearances as much as possible. If he was even on the right track.

"Exactly how dexterous are you with your fingers, Mrs. MacIntyre?" he asked.

"What . . . what do you mean?" Her

eyes wide, she tried to stare him down.

"I suspect that your husband is running some sort of scam here, and that you are involved. Then he disappeared, and you're worried about what's happened to him. Is he talking to the police? Has someone harmed him? You need to know."

Mrs. Mac twisted her hands in the straps of her purse and wouldn't look at him.

"Is what I tell you confidential? Like with a priest or a lawyer?" she asked.

"No. Not really. If there is any criminal act involved, I have to report it."

She stood up abruptly, hands still working the purse strap. "I have nothing more to say to you, then, Mr. High. Thank you for letting me know that you saw my husband this morning. I won't be needing your services any longer."

She turned to leave, but was stopped by a policeman. She looked back helplessly at Phil as she was led away. He almost felt sorry for her.

Then another cop approached him. She was quite pleasant to look at, so Phil looked. She frowned at him.

"I'm Detective Anderson. Please come this way. I understand you're the person who found the body."

"Yeah."

The detective led Phil to an unleased store where some desks and chairs had been placed in the corners. Mrs. Mac was talking to the officer who had come to get her, and Detective Anderson and Phil sat in the opposite corner.

Detective Anderson led Phil through some routine questions about finding the body. Then she said, "We hear that you were running through the mall earlier today, chasing a man who had a bad scar on his face. Want to tell me about that?" He'd never noticed before how piercing green eyes could be. He wondered if she disliked how plump and kissable her lips were when she was detecting. He knew he was reacting as most men must—like an idiot.

"An old friend," Phil said. "Hadn't seen him in years. Wanted to catch up with him, but lost him in the crowd."

"When you fell down."

"Yeah, there was that."

"Then you were talking to a woman just before I came to get you. Quite earnestly and quite quietly."

"Also an old friend."

Anderson gave him a doubtful look and twisted a stray lock of blond hair in her slim fingers. "Her name?"

"Cary MacIntyre."

"Name of the old friend you were chasing?"

"Um, Jimmy MacIntyre."

Anderson's look was falsely incredulous. "Mrs. MacIntyre hired you to find Mr. MacIntyre, right?"

"I can see," said Phil gravely, "why you were promoted to Detective, Detective. Such powerful reasoning ability."

"Don't get cute with me, Mr. High. I'll have your license and your hide."

Phil sighed. Since there was a murder involved, and probably another crime, he came clean. "Okay. Yes, Mrs. MacIntyre hired me to find Mr. MacIntyre. She said she made a report to the police but they weren't doing much."

The detective wrote something down on a piece of paper and signaled one of the other officers to come over. She handed him the paper. "Check these two out, and see if she made a missing persons report on him. ASAP."

"Yes, ma'am."

As the officer turned away, Detective Anderson gave Phil a steely glare. "What did you find out about the MacIntyre's?"
Phil shifted to get more comfortable in the small chair. Both his own bulk and that of the Santa suit got in his way. "Neither has a record, as far as I could determine. I could find no trace of him until I saw him this morning. His wife claims that he knew she went to the gym every morning, so he wouldn't worry that she'd see him here. I am not sure that he knew I was trying to run him down, but I suspect he did know because when I fell, then got up, he was nowhere to be found. I imagine he ducked into a store and

hid. I also suspect that there's some sort of scam involving Santa's Corner. Maybe Larry found out what it was, and he was murdered. At this point, I suspect everyone from the elf, Ginny Brown, to the mall manager, Ingrid Scruggs."

Detective Anderson looked at Phil in astonishment. "I didn't think threats would work," she said.

"They don't. Murder is serious business, and although Larry was quite a drinker—I assume you knew that?"

She shook her head and made a note on her pad.

"I liked Larry, and no one had the right to murder him. You have resources I don't have, so perhaps my telling you everything I know will help clear this up."

"I see. Is that all you have to tell me?"

"That's all of it. I hope you find the scum who did this, Detective. And yes, I'd look long and hard at Jimmy MacIntyre and his wife."

The officer came over to tell Detective Anderson that there had been no missing person report made on a Jimmy or James MacIntyre and neither he nor Mrs. MacIntyre had an priors.

Phil and the detective exchanged glances, then both stood up and shook hands. Detective Anderson gave Phil one of her business cards in case he thought of anything else.

Phil wandered out to the mall floor and spotted Ingrid standing off to the side, watching all the activity.

"You have any idea who did this?" Ingrid asked. She gave him a look which said she put him at the top of her suspect list.

"I figured it was you," Phil said with a straight face.

"Don't be ridiculous."

Of course Ingrid wouldn't murder Santa; it would tarnish her image. "You walk around here a lot. Did you see anything unusual going on in the line?"

"No. Well, maybe. I don't know."

He'd never seen Ingrid so indecisive before. "Well, which is it? What did you see?"

"Occasionally I'd see someone without a child hanging around. She looked something like that woman you were talking to earlier. Sometimes there was a man with her. He had a rather visible scar on his face. He'd leave, and she's stay. But I never really saw her do anything. I think once she noticed me watching her, and she left right away. After that she always left if she saw me."

"You get any reports about alleged crimes committed in the mall, right?"

"Yes." Ingrid raised her eyebrows at him.

"Any increase lately? How about pocket picking?"

"There has been an increase, but there always is this time of year. Holiday spirit, or spirits, you know," she said with a wry grin. Ingrid told a joke? Phil looked at her in astonishment.

"Okay," he said. "No unusual increase this year, then?"

"Not really. The only odd thing is that the police have come back to me with the information that several of the people who reported their wallets stolen here this year have also have also been the victims of identity theft."

"Oh ho," Santa said.

Ingrid gave him a horrified look.

Phil nodded. "While waiting in line. Somehow Larry caught on. The problem will be proving it. Come on, we need to talk to a certain Detective Anderson."

The crowd had thinned out, and as they walked to the store, Phil noticed Ginny and gestured for her to join them.

"What are we going to do about Santa's Corner?" she asked Ingrid.

"Closed for tonight. I'll have to talk to the police about it."

"I think they'll probably want this section of the mall cordoned off for a few days," Phil said. "We may have to relocate, but I think we should open it again. Better for business, right, Ingrid?"

"Well, yes."

They entered the shop where witnesses were still being interviewed and waited for Detective Anderson to finish with a woman who grasped a squalling baby in her lap and held tightly to a little boy's hand. He appeared to be around five years old. Mom looked frazzled and unhappy.

"I tell you, I didn't see anything, I don't know anything, and I need to get these kids home and fed. Are you a mother?"

"Uh, no."

"I didn't think so. Why don't you hold the baby while we finish this interview?"

Phil hid a smile behind his hand. Detective Anderson noticed the three of them and frowned.

"You can go now," she said.

"Thanks so much," the woman said, rising awkwardly while clasping the baby to her chest. "Shh. Shh," she said as she left the store, tugging on the little boy's hand.

Phil filled the detective in on what he had found out from Ingrid. Anderson brusquely thanked him and said goodbye.

"Detective, I was thinking," Phil said.

She quirked an eyebrow at him.

"Maybe we could set a trap. You will let us set up Santa's Corner somewhere else in the mall, right?"

"Yes. Sure."

"Maybe you could have some people scattered around, watching."

"I'll consider the idea. Thank you again, Mr. High, for your time."

"Sure," Phil said, and the three of them left.

"She didn't seem to keen on your idea," Ginny said.

"No, she didn't," Phil said. "But I bet she does it anyway, just in case."

Ingrid snorted. "Not likely whoever was doing this would come back and do it some more."

"You never know," Phil said. "Routine, get in a rut, do the familiar. And perhaps keep an eye on how things are going with the investigation."

"Huh," Ingrid said. *Charming as always*, Phil thought.

"I'm going to get out of this suit and go home," he said. "It's been a long day."

Phil changed as quickly as he could, stuffed the Santa suit into his locker, and rushed out to the part of the parking lot where the mall employees usually parked, hoping to see Ginny's car still there. It was. The air was crisp and cold, as Phil thought it should be this time of year, but he was glad it wasn't storming.

Once settled behind the wheel of his own Honda Civic, he pulled out Detective Anderson's business card and punched her number into his cell, saving it under "Snooty Det," sure he'd be able to remember that if the going got tough. Then he hunkered down and waited for Ginny.

Ginny didn't even glance his way when she came out. He'd never seen her out of her elf suit, and she looked entirely different. She wore a short black and white figured skirt and tight t-shirt under her open dark green wool, duster-length coat. Black boots completed the outfit. When she climbed into her new Volkswagen, her skirt hiked up so much that Phil had to look away. He was having a hard time reconciling the two images of her—the sophisticated siren and the innocent elf. Out of the elf suit, she looked like someone else he knew, but he couldn't think who. She'd been acting strangely today, and he had a hunch she knew something about all that was going on.

Phil followed Ginny to a middle-class neighborhood lined with leafless trees. He hoped she wasn't simply going home. She pulled into a driveway and around to the back, probably to park in a garage. Phil made a sound of disgust.

He noted the address, and something rang a bell in his brain. It was the address Mrs. Mac had given him when she hired him. She had to give him a good address because he could easily match the phone number to it. And, good detective that he was, he had cross-checked them.

Phil climbed out of his car and closed the door carefully so it wouldn't make a sound. He crept around to the back the house, looking in windows as he went. At the back door, he heard raised voices. He was able to see Jimmy Mac by looking through a slit in the curtains on the door window.

"I can't believe how badly both of you

handled everything. First you—" Jimmy Mac's arm stretched with pointed finger to someone Phil couldn't see, "go to a Private Eye. What were you thinking?"

"We didn't know where you were!" Mrs. Mac's voice was high and strained. "Where were you? We were worried and scared."

"I had some things to take care of. I was thinking of expanding the business."

"Why were you at the mall this afternoon? Phil saw you there."

"Oh, you're on a first-name basis with this P.I.?

"For heaven's sake, don't get all jealous on me now. Why were you there?"

"I was done with business and came to check on Ginny."

Ginny said, "You could have let us know. Why are you always so secretive?" And Phil High knew who Ginny looked like—her mother, Cary MacIntyre.

"I have my reasons. And you! Who the hell told you to murder Larry? I would have handled it."

"We didn't know where you were, Dad! I was afraid he'd go to the police."

"So what if he had? A blackmailing drunk. They would have found no proof. Now we're gonna have to get out of here. Start packing, the both of you."

Phil crept back to his car, shocked about Ginny being Larry's murderer—he'd felt sure it had been Jimmy Mac—and called the

MacIntyre's number.

When the answering machine picked up, he said, "This is Santa Claus. I see Ginny got home okay." He hung up.

Shortly, the front door opened, and Jimmy MacIntyre stood there, looking around. He spotted Phil's car and sprinted toward it. When Phil saw the gun in Jimmy Mac's hand, he quickly started the engine and floored it. Jimmy got off two shots, one of which went through the back window and the windshield, barely missing Phil's head. *Dumb move, Santa,* Phil told himself. But he'd wanted the MacIntyre's to feel a sense of urgency about getting away.

When he outpaced Jimmy, he pulled over, not surprised to see his hands shaking. He called Snooty Det and told her what had happened.

"We're on it," she said.

When he heard the sirens, he drove back to the MacIntyre house and waited. After awhile, he watched the three of them taken away in handcuffs.

Detective Anderson came over to where Phil was leaning against his car. "We found wallets, IDs, and fake IDs. Fortunately they decided to flee, so they had taken everything out of hiding."

"Almost spoils Christmas, doesn't it?" Santa said. "I even feel sorry for Ingrid. Larry's dead, and Ginny's off to jail. I'm trying to imagine Ingrid in an elf suit." He shuddered and grinned. "I suppose Ginny came right home to tell her parents about the plan to stake out Santa's Corner."

"Yeah, Phil. You made some good moves, I admit. They're going away for a long time. I guarantee it. And some folks will have a very happy Christmas, getting their identities back and cleared, thanks to Santa."

"Ho, ho, ho," Santa said.

Copyright ©2007 Jan Christensen

Mystery on Capitol Street
A Hannibal Jones Short Story
Austin S. Camacho

There was no reason to think the guy wrapped in a blanket needed killing but Hannibal very nearly finished him that night.

Neither the light snow nor the ugly traffic two days before Christmas was any excuse for his bad judgment. His investigation in Baltimore yielded a nice fee that would let him get his girl Cindy something really nice for Christmas this year. But by midnight his brain was feeling mushy.

He wanted to get home that night so that he would have all of Christmas Eve day to search for the perfect thing. But he screwed up and went west on the beltway when he should have gone east. That's what led him off the Beltway at the first exit and into the heart of The District heading south.

Groggy and frustrated, racing down North Capital Street trying to beat a red light, he suddenly found a man framed in his headlights. It was a white guy with pale and sickly skin, wrapped in a blanket for want of a coat. One of the city's many homeless, Hannibal figured, unsteady on his feet and reacting way too slowly. Hannibal yanked the wheel hard right and floored the Volvo's brake pedal. He didn't miss the man by much, and didn't miss the fire hydrant at all. The impact wasn't enough to pop his air bags, but his heart spasmed as he realized he could have crushed the stranger in the street. He watched the man stagger off into Rock Creek Cemetery and tried to catch his breath.

By the time his near victim was lost behind the sheet of drifting snow, Hannibal had accepted the facts. He was too tired to drive home safely. He managed a three-point turn and drove back to a motel he passed a couple of blocks earlier.

The Capitol Inn motel was a generic but homey little place. The thin young desk clerk with the afro jumped when Hannibal walked in. The tee shirt under his silver angel medallion marked him as a college kid.

"Relax," Hannibal said. "I'm just looking for a room."

The kid paused, staring. Hannibal figured he'd never seen a black man with hazel eyes before.

Hannibal said, "They're real, and I'm beat. A room, please?"

"Sorry, man," the desk clerk said. "We're all full up. Not one vacancy."

"No room at the inn, eh? I think I've heard that story before. Come on, man, help a brother out. If you can't find me a bed I'll have to crash right here in the lobby, and that chair don't look none too comfortable."

"We can't have that, can we?" A tall brunette with high Latin cheek bones stepped in behind Hannibal. Even under the black wool coat he could see that her figure was robust but not out of control.

"But Mrs. Cruz, every room is booked," the desk clerk said. "Christmas rush and all that."

"Maybe, Mitchell, but this is my motel and I won't turn this man away," she said. "What if he gets into an accident on his way home? Sir, we have a small attic room that we don't usually rent out but it does have a bed and a dresser. You can have it for a reduced rate."

Hannibal matched her warm smile with one of his own and reached for his credit card.

***

After a short but sound sleep, Hannibal was up and out of his little room by six. He took the stairs down but on the second floor he noticed red drops on the stairs. He wanted to get home, but he was a detective by nature and could no more ignore a possible blood trail than most people could drive past an accident without slowing down to look. He followed the red spots down the hall toward the sounds of a woman's gentle sobbing.

Silent steps carried him through the open door to stand behind the maid. She was kneeling on the thin carpet, scrubbing hard while crying softly.

"You can't get blood out that way," Hannibal said. "Even if you can't see it, the forensics boys will find it."

The girl leaped to her feet. She was below thirty and beyond pretty, with straight brown hair styled to caress her face. Eyes the color of the ocean at high tide stretched wide and her lower lip quivered. The uniform didn't conceal her abundant curves.

"Who are you?"

Before Hannibal could answer, Mrs. Cruz leaned in the door. "Mr. Jones is a guest, Tina. You are an early riser, Mr. Jones."

"Occupational hazard," Hannibal said. "Want to tell me what happened in here?"

"Nothing to concern yourself about," Mrs. Cruz said. "One of the guests got a little wild. There was an accident. I think he hurt himself."

"Real careless," Hannibal said, glancing from the maid to the hotel owner. "Did he survive his little accident?"

The older woman's laugh was high and light. "I assure you he was healthy when he checked out. Did you sleep well?"

"Better than the last guy in this room I bet," Hannibal said. "But you don't need me poking around in your business, and I need to get home."

Hannibal followed Mrs. Cruz to the front desk to check out.

"The maid is your daughter?" he asked.

"How did you know?"

"She has your hair. And is blessed with your figure. Take a word of advice, Mrs. Cruz?"

She rested an elbow on the desk and slipped her chin onto it. "Judith. Please."

"All right, Judith. Accidents like that go away faster if you show you've nothing to hide. Call the police and tell them about it. As shaken as your daughter was cleaning up a stranger's blood, she won't do well under police questioning."

Judith nodded and smiled. "Do you have a wife, Mr. Jones? A lover?"

"I have someone, yes."

"Then take a word of advice from me. It is Christmas Eve. Don't think about our troubles. Think about what she would want you to be doing now."

***

Listening to his tires crunching over the half inch of snow, Hannibal was thinking just that. Cindy would want him to take responsibility for his own actions. So he parked just two blocks away and walked into the Rock Creek Cemetery. Hannibal wanted to find the man he almost ran over. If he spent the night in the cemetery, Hannibal would buy him a decent breakfast, and maybe a second hand coat.

He knew he was too late as soon as he spotted the man curled up under a tree. Hannibal could see his own breath in the crisp morning air, but not the other man's. Fingers pressed against the stranger's neck confirmed his death, but a close look dispelled another assumption. He was too well groomed to be homeless. Lipstick on his mouth and cheek implied that he had not spent the entire night alone. The blanket wrapped around him was identical to the one Hannibal had slept under the night before, except for the dark stain from blood that had leaked from a bullet wound in the man's abdomen.

"You came pretty far, considering you were gut shot," Hannibal said. The man's pockets yielded no wallet, but Hannibal did find two small boxes: a matchbox from a restaurant called Ceiba and a gift box containing a white gold pendant of the name "Belinda" in script. *They might be enough*, he thought, *to find whoever was missing this man on Christmas Eve.*

***

Judith Cruz greeted Hannibal when he walked back into the lobby. "Mr. Jones, you're back. What can I do for you now?"

"You can take my advice seriously," Hannibal said. "Your accident prone guest is only a couple blocks down the street, wrapped in one of your blankets. I've already told the cops he was shot here. When they arrive you should be ready to tell them what happened. You could start by telling me."

Judith only hesitated for a second. "I was still at the theater when it happened. After you went to bed, Mitchell told me that the man got drunk and shot himself, then walked out of the hotel. I didn't want to get involved but I suppose I have no choice now."

Hannibal rolled his eyes. "Shot himself. Right. What happened to the girl?"

"Girl?"

"He was with a girl last night. Trust me."

Judith turned to the small screen behind the desk and tapped the keyboard. Her brows knit, then relaxed. "No, he checked in alone. Bo D'Agostino of Arlington, Virginia. Of course, he could have had company later. I also see that you're a private detective. Interesting."

"In what way?"

She smiled into Hannibal's lenses. "That dead man could be a fugitive you were tailing. You could have followed him here."

"But I wasn't"

She pulled a stack of bills out of the drawer and pushed them toward him. "But, you could have been."

Hannibal pushed her hand back toward her. "Sorry. I don't invent jobs, and I only get paid for real ones."

"Then let's make it real," Judith said. "I'll pay you to find out who shot a guest in my hotel."

Hannibal thought there was a good chance she wouldn't want to know, but finding the truth fit his goals at the time.

"Fine. And if Mitchell signed him in, that's who I need to talk to first."

***

Mitchell's apartment was across the

street from the hotel. Mitchell sat in a corner of his worn sofa and offered Hannibal a kitchen chair. He had changed to a fresh tee shirt but the two-inch silver angel medal still hung from his neck. His eyes went to the floor when Hannibal questioned him.

"He must have checked in around 10, and checked out around 12:30 or so."

"Checked out?" Hannibal asked. "You saw him leave. Wounded like that?"

Mitchell blanched. "Look, I didn't see what happened, okay? I heard a shot, I went upstairs. He was standing there, holding a gun, wrapped in a blanket. He went down the stairs. I checked him out after he left."

"Him? Or them? What about the girl?"

Mitchell's fingers went up through his afro. "Okay, okay. Yeah they came together. But she left before him. I saw him leave but she was already gone."

"So she's either the killer or a witness. What did this woman look like?"

Mitchell's eyes went up to his left as if he was looking for something inside his head. "She was tall. Real tall. White girl, blonde hair, blue eyes, um, kind of on the heavy side. You going to try to find her?"

"Well I do have an idea where to look."

***

Ceiba, the name on the matchbox, turned out to be the name of a Latin American tree, and a restaurant that served Latin food. The greeter looked like he could play Alfred in the next Batman movie.

"I'm working a missing person case," Hannibal said, flashing his credentials. "Can your reservations computer tell me the last time a guy named Bo D'Agostino ate here? The woman he was with has gone missing."

The Alfred look-alike pushed buttons on a small console. "Mr. D'Agostino is a regular here, and as it happens he dined with us last night. Party of two."

"Know anything about the girl, Belinda? Tall, blonde type?"

The greeter's eyes clouded and he shook his head. "Belinda has been here many times with Mr. D'Agostino, but that certainly doesn't describe her. Ms. Pearl is quite petite."

"Okay, if you say so. Where do I go to find this petite little thing?"

"That I can't tell you," the greeter said. "But I can tell you where to find Mr. D'Agostino. He'll be preparing for the Christmas Eve rush at his own club." He flipped through a file box and pulled out a business card. Hannibal accepted it, not wanting to tell the man that he was wrong about knowing where to find D'Agostino.

***

The Kappa Club must have been a popular fraternity hangout at one time, Hannibal guessed, or else that Greek letter carried some meaning he wasn't aware of. Barely twenty minutes from downtown Washington, the little club was trying to be a honky-tonk bar with its rustic décor and beer aroma and posters of the country acts that played there every night. The barmaid in denims and cowboy hat was standing on a table to hang even more tinsel from the rafters. She smiled when he entered so he decided to try the direct approach.

"Afternoon. I'm looking for Belinda. Need to return this." He dangled the name pendant in the air.

"Belinda?" the barmaid echoed. "Mr. D's girl? She took off more than a month ago. Haven't seen her since." Then she hopped down to the floor, leaned close and lowered her voice. "And if you've seen her since, I'd keep it to myself. If Mr. D knew another guy got close enough to get her jewelry off her…"

"Can I help you?" The man walking from the back was tall and beefy man with ruddy skin and a bulbous, veined nose. He wore a western shirt and pointed boots, but his voice was more New Jersey than Texas. "I'm Roy McCraney, the owner."

"Hannibal Jones, private investigator. You must be D'Agostino's partner and, yes, maybe you can help me."

McCraney noticed the pendant in Hannibal's hand and seemed to make a connection. "Oh. I see. We need to talk in private, Mr. Jones. Join me in my office."

McCraney led Hannibal into a small back room, stepped behind the desk and pushed an intercom button.

"Tell Blane to get in here, and bring Rod with him." Then he looked up at Hannibal. "Did she kill him, or did you?"

"I don't understand," Hannibal said.

"Oh, I think it's pretty clear," McCraney said. "You're the guy with evidence that you've seen Belinda," McCraney said. "I'm the guy who wants to know where the bitch is. So you're here either to sell that information or blackmail me. And Blane there behind you? He's the guy with the gun. Now put your hands on the desk."

Hannibal barely had time to feel stupid before he felt the impact on the back of his skull and the weightless feeling took over.

***

He felt even stupider when he awoke, handcuffed to a chair. McCraney and Blane were standing behind the desk deep in conversation.

"It don't matter," McCraney said, looking up at Blane. "She's a threat as long as she's alive to testify. I can't do hard time for a drug rap."

"My boys found her once, we can do it again, boss."

So they were drug dealers, Hannibal thought. Maybe D'Agostino did need killing after all. Aloud he said, "So she was on the run. I guess your partner really was sweet on her, and went after her to bring her home for Christmas."

"You already knew that," McCraney

said. "You're in it with her. That's why she sent you with that calling card."

Hannibal shook his head. "Actually I took this off D'Agostino's body. I guess they've already notified you of his death. You don't look too broke up about your loss."

"Shut up," McCraney said. "Bo was a good man. Just too bad he fell for the hired help. She broke his heart when she ran off, but to me she was just a security threat. Now where the hell is she?"

"Idiot, I'm looking for her too," Hannibal said. "I don't know what she knows about your drug operation, but it must be good. Now, I can give her to the cops, or, for the right price I can give her to you."

"Or I can put a bullet in your dome," Blane said.

"Yeah, and then you'd never see her again until you faced her in court," Hannibal said. "You know I'll find her. After all, I found you before the cops even identified D'Agostino's body."

McCraney leaned back against the desk. "You'd give her up?"

"Sure, I'd give her up. For five grand."

Hannibal guessed that McCraney's opinion of private detectives was pretty low. After a little thought, McCraney gestured for Blane to open the cuffs. "We can do business. What do you need?"

Hannibal stood up and patted his empty holster. "I'll need my gun back, and a picture of the girl."

McCraney fished a photo of Belinda out of his desk. Then he picked up Hannibal's gun but dropped the magazine before handing it over. "I assume you've got more bullets," he said.

Hannibal slipped his gun into its holster and said, "I'll be in touch."

Back on the Beltway it took Hannibal a while to spot the car he knew would be following him, and several more minutes to lose it in The District's dense traffic. When he was sure he had shaken the tail he raced back to the Capitol Inn. He marched up to the counter wearing an expression that froze Judith Cruz in her place.

"Where is she?"

"Where is who?"

"Belinda, the woman Bo D'Agostino came in here with," Hannibal said, slapping the photo he got from McCraney down on the counter, "otherwise known as your daughter Tina."

Judith's mouth worked but nothing came out, so Hannibal continued. "I figure she changed her name to protect you, or maybe so you wouldn't find out she was sleeping with a gangster, but I'm sure you know now."

Tears began to roll from Judith's eyes. "She didn't know what she was getting into. When she found out, she left him. She was hiding in shame up north, but somehow he found her. He kidnapped her, was forcing her to go back with him."

"Really? So she brought him here?"

"He didn't know who I was. She convinced him to stop for the night on their way back to his place. She came here hoping I could save her."

"Well, at least now I understand why Mitchell didn't want anyone to know D'Agostino had a girl with him. Changing from guest to employee made Tina disappear. And if he gave the police the same description he gave me for the mystery girl they could look for that girl forever. But D'Agostino's partner will never stop looking for her. You've got to let me help her."

"Tina told me she knew things, details of a drug business that could get her killed. She left right after the police did. No telling where she'll go to hide."

"Maybe, but her first stop is pretty obvious."

Hannibal raced across the street, almost slipping on the thin layer of white. When Mitchell opened the door light flashed into Hannibal's eyes from the silver angel medallion.

"Did Tina give you that?" Hannibal asked. When Mitchell looked down at the medal, Hannibal elbowed him aside and burst into the room. He stopped a few steps in, staring down the barrel of the gun Tina was pointing at him.

"That belongs to Bo, doesn't it?"

Hannibal asked. "You killed him with his own piece."

"No, I shot him," Mitchell said, moving to stand beside Tina. "I could see when they came in that she didn't want him to know I knew her. She looked so scared. I couldn't let him take her back, so I sneaked into the room while he was in the bathroom and grabbed his gun. When he came out I shot him and ran."

"That's why you looked so spooked when I showed up, and why you didn't want anybody coming in. But Tina's mother came in right behind me, and she had no idea what was going on. I'm guessing you didn't plan the killing, Tina. You just did what people do when they're scared. You ran home."

"Bo treated me nice at first," Tina said, the gun shaking in her hand. "But then he started to act like he owned me. And when I saw they were dealing drugs I just had to get away. But I need to stay on the run. Those people will never stop chasing me."

"There's a better way, Tina," Hannibal said. "I called a cop friend of mine in Virginia on my way here. He can take you into protective custody. He can keep you safe until McCraney's brought to justice. From what I got out of him, your testimony is enough to put him in jail for a long time."

"Be easier to shoot you," she said, pointing the pistol with both hands.

"Sure," Hannibal said. "Then you'd have McCraney *and* the cops chasing you. My way, you can come out of this on the side of the good guys. Besides, you're no killer. It took you all night to be able to face cleaning up the blood of the man you had been sleeping with. Now put down the gun."

"He's right," Mitchell said. "Running ain't the answer. Besides, I can't let you just disappear out of my life again. I want you home for Christmas."

Mitchell took the pistol out of Tina's hand and tossed it on the sofa. She sighed with relief; and Hannibal felt his first genuine smile of the day.

"Thanks, chump," Blane said. Hannibal spun to see the mobster's form filling the doorway, his gun held forward.

"Where the hell did you come from?"

"Got lucky," Blane said, stepping inside. "You lost me on The Beltway, but I couldn't go back and tell the boss. I didn't know what else to do, so I went to the spot where they found Mr. D's body. I was almost there when I saw you running across the street."

"Okay, you got me," Hannibal said. "Now what? I can't let you take the girl back."

"Don't want to," Blane said.

A lot happened in the next two seconds. Blane aimed at Tina. Hannibal dropped toward the sofa. Mitchell dived in front of Tina. Blane fired. Mitchell fell to the floor. Blane swung his gun toward Hannibal, who grabbed the discarded gun but couldn't bring it on line before another shot roared in the room. Then Blane dropped to his knees and pitched forward.

Standing behind Blane, Fairfax Country police detective Orson Rissik said, "Sorry I wasn't here sooner."

Hannibal looked at Rissik's smoking service revolver, and then sprang to Mitchell's still form. While Tina cradled the young man's head Hannibal ripped his tee shirt open, prepared to apply pressure to a bullet wound. Instead he found only a broad bruise.

"One of the boys is calling an ambulance now," Rissik said, leading three uniforms into the room. "He's mighty lucky to still be breathing."

"Luckier than you can guess," Hannibal said. He held up the mangled angel medallion. "This apparently deflected the slug. I wouldn't have believed it if I didn't see it with my own eyes."

"Well, it is the season for miracles," Rissik said. "But the girl's mighty lucky too, that you happened to be around to keep her from making even more stupid mistakes."

Tina faced Rissik bravely. "If he told you everything, then I guess Mitchell is under arrest, huh?"

"Well, I'm betting he'll spend the night in a hospital with a broken rib or two," Rissik said, "But after that, I don't think he'll have any trouble convincing a jury that D'Agostino's death was justified to save a kidnapped girl."

"What about the protective custody?" Hannibal asked. "Blane's boss is determined."

"He's also in jail," Rissik said. "I had him picked up before I left to meet you at the hotel. So I think we can protect Ms. Cruz well enough until his trial without locking her away. Besides, I kind of think she'd rather be home for Christmas, don't you?"

Copyright ©2007 Austin Camacho

The Christmas Cutout Caper
Tony Burton

Billy, Wesley, Larry and Mike called themselves "The Fantastic Four," but to most adults around town they were known by other names, most of them not bearing repeating in polite company. And they'd earned the names, too.

Case in point: two years ago, at the town's Founder's Day celebration, they decked out the brand-new statue of Colonel J. T. Swensen in a sequined bikini, fastened to the statue with epoxy. Since the Colonel is the Famous Celebrity after whom the town is named, this caused no small amount of angst when the statue was unveiled with a flourish before the town and Press.

Then there was the time they dumped two hundred boxes of fruit gelatin mix in the courthouse fountain. And who can forget the time they "borrowed" about 10,000 crickets from a local bait wholesaler and turned them loose in the high school the morning of the last day of school. Oh and there's the… well, you get the idea.

Nevertheless, it had been about a year since they had done anything dastardly, and a few of the adults were starting to breathe easier when any sort of special occasion rolled around. Halloween passed without any exploding pumpkins or diarrhea-inducing candies. Thanksgiving came and went without anything obscene being done to turkeys.

Pastor Grady Snow of the Swensen Lutheran Church proudly supervised the construction of the large Christmas display on the front lawn of the church. For six years Pastor Snow had shepherded the flock and he was the one who started the tradition of the life-sized crèche. A few of the more artistic ladies had wrangled their husbands and boyfriends into creating plywood cutouts in the shape of shepherds, the Virgin Mary, Joseph, and the Magi, while they busied themselves with adorning the saintly plywood figures with paint, tinsel and fabric.

Someone also located a few large used plastic replicas of animals which they purchased (at a discount) from a circus supplier in Winnetka. They repainted the zebras into donkeys and modified the giraffe into a camel, which greatly complimented the scene. Finally, a large faux rooster from ValueMart Garden Center stood at the head of the manger, while the pinewood holy parents, shepherds and wise men looked on adoringly at the doll nestled in the hay. The result was rather handsome, from a reasonable distance.

Jeannette Amberle, president of the Ladies Aid, finished adjusting the gold lamé draped on a plywood wise man, and stood back with her fists on her ample hips, admiring her handiwork.

"Beautiful, Mrs. Amberle, just lovely," gushed Pastor Snow. "I've never seen a truer representation of Melchior, Balthazar and Gaspar!" He stood with hands clasped together. "All the ladies have worked miracles with the crèche figures this year!"

Inez Johnson hove herself into view from behind the *faux* stable, grunting as she pulled at the giraffe/camel. "What in the *world* made this thing so heavy?" she grumbled. The rope tightened and creaked as she leaned her considerable bulk into the pull, but she overcame friction and the makeshift camel slid forward about a foot. Pastor Snow hurried forward.

"Here, let me help you with that, Mrs. Johnson. I asked Mr. Larson to pour some sand into the plastic animals this year, after last year's winds blew them all over the place. But I thought he would have waited… urrgh!… until after we had them situated… ungh!… before pouring it in… oofda! There," he said, panting. He patted the artificial animal's hump, made of painted car-body repair compound. "Let's leave it right here."

They all stepped back to the salt-encrusted sidewalk to admire their handiwork. Since today was December 1, tonight's illuminated display would be the first of the season, to continue through the last day of December. The floodlights were all in place, with appropriately colored lenses over the lights to evoke the proper mood when the time came.

"Ladies, let us all go into the fellowship hall. Helena has prepared some coffee and sugar cookies. It's cold out, and we have all been working hard." With a sweeping gesture of both arms, he led the little group into the church, where they warmed both their insides and their outsides.

At 6:00 PM, the floodlights bathed the crèche in a beautiful, multicolored glow. Hidden speakers inside the false stable poured out a constant flow of music considered by the pastor to be most representative of the music of the heavenly host. It was never clear to anyone where Andy Williams, Robert Goulet and Bing Crosby fit in with the heavenly host, but the music was nice, anyway.

The cars began cruising by soon afterward, slowing to let both children and the older folks goggle at the show. The air was filled with "oohs!", "ahhhs!" and carbon monoxide. Pastor Snow and his wife, Helena, stood at the window of the parsonage across the street and watched with pride as the procession slowed, and camera flash after camera flash illuminated the scene of the moment of God's incarnation.

But something alien and heathenish penetrated their double-paned windows. The pounding bass and atonal chanting of rap music replaced the plaintive strains of "Do You Hear What I Hear." A large blue pickup with gigantic, thumping speakers in the back eased up, stopping in front of the Christmas crèche. The windows between the pastor and the pickup truck vibrated, and his cup of tea sitting on the windowsill had ripples forming in its surface. Helena stepped back, face strained and forehead marked with lines denoting a combination of pain and irritation. Andy William's voice could no longer be heard—only the thumping bass and voices of young men "gettin' jiggy wid it." The truck belonged to Mike Pearce, one of the Fantastic Four.

After an outrageous ten minutes of this, Pastor Snow donned his coat and was about to ask the young pagans to move along. "Wait, honey!" his wife called, "They're leaving, thank God!" Indeed, the noisy truck was pulling away from the curb, and other cars without interfering noise were pulling up to take their place. Once more the camera flashes began, and all was well.

At midnight, Pastor Snow walked across the street to the church to turn off the music and all but one floodlight, the one shining directly on the cutouts of the Holy Family. He smiled as he walked back to his warm home, breath hanging in the chilled air. Even with the little brush with paganism earlier in the evening, the first night had been a success.

The next morning, Helena was up bright and early to fix her husband's favorite breakfast, poached eggs and hash browns. In a short while he came downstairs, adorned in slacks and a festive holiday sweater.

She beamed at him as she sat the plate and a cup of coffee, in front her husband. "You wore the Christmas sweater I knitted for you, Grady! How lovely!" He smiled in response, and the two lopsided 100% acrylic snowmen leered up at her from his chest. She planted a kiss on his brow and went to get her own coffee.

They quickly disposed of breakfast, with some talk about the schedule for the coming day, and Grady went to stand by the window with his coffee. There was a light snow beginning to fall, just as the weather person on the clock radio had said there would be. *It's comforting,* he thought, *that some things are reliable.* He smiled out at the dancing snowflakes falling on his front lawn, on the sidewalk and on the crèche across the road.

Grady almost choked and blew heavily sugared coffee all over the window in front of him. Little dots of coffee freckled the snowmen on his holiday sweater. His breath fogged the window, so he frantically rubbed it away to check the view once more. He was right.

Helena came running over as quickly as her fuzzy slippers would let her. "What's the matter, honey? Burn your tongue?" He shook his head, voicelessly pointing at the window. She stared at the window, frowning in puzzlement. "What is it, dear? I don't under… oh, my God!" She grabbed Grady by the arm, and spilled the remainder of his coffee all over the front of his sweater. The snowmen on his chest now looked like Springer Spaniels, brown and white blotched.

The Christmas crèche figures were gone. Missing. Vanished. The animals were there, along the manger, baby Jesus and the little stable made of log slabs and old packing crate wood, but all the beautifully decorated plywood figures were gone. No Mary, no Joseph, no shepherds nor magi were on the lawn.

Grady shook himself free from Helena's grasp and said, "Call the constable! I'm going over there to see if I can see any traces of them!" He ran to the door and jammed his feet into his boots without tying the laces, while Helena ran to the kitchen and grabbed the phone.

Officer Olafsen arrived within minutes. In fact, Grady had only made one circuit of the church property by the time Officer Olafsen stepped out of his patrol vehicle. The blue and red lights made the tinseled star above the stable glitter, but it was a poor show compared to how it had looked with all the plywood figures. Grady was standing in front of the stable, staring down at the plastic Child in the manger, his lips moving soundlessly.

Officer Olafsen saw what was happening, and removed his hat respectfully as he neared the pastor. He didn't want to interrupt the pastor at prayer, but Grady was oblivious to his approach. When the officer was within a couple of feet, he made out the pastor's whispered words, "... blast the little heathen monsters! I hope they rot in the pits of..." The officer's eyes grew wider, but he replaced his hat and cleared his throat. Grady whirled, his eyes brimming with tears.

"They're gone, Olie! They've been stolen!" Grady was Officer Olafsen's minister, so he got away with calling him Olie. "It was those young sons of... those conniving little bast... I mean..."

"The Fantastic Four, you mean?" Olie asked.

"YES!" Grady shouted, then looked shamefaced. "I'm sorry, Olie. I'll calm down. They came by here last night, about 8:45 or so. They sat in front of the crèche for a long time, probably fifteen minutes at least, blaring away with that stupid music they listen to, so loud we couldn't hear Bing or Andy or *any* of the Christmas favorites!"

Olie's face grew grim, and his blonde eyebrows drew together. "Did they do anything else? Get out and look at the figures, or anything suspicious?"

Grady shook his head. "No, they just disturbed the peace and caused a backup in the normal flow of people driving by the Christmas crèche. But you *know* how they are, Olie!"

Olie sighed. Indeed, he knew how they were. His son Thor occasionally hung out with Billy Anderson, and Olie had warned him more than once about lying down with dogs and picking up fleas. But Thor knew it all—at nineteen they do—and only grinned at the warnings. Olie looked around at the ground, where the light snowfall of the morning had dusted everything.

"But what would they do with them, Pastor?" he asked. "Why would they take...." but he stopped. It was well-known that *those* boys needed no reason, other than boredom and sheer meanness.

"I'll get on it, Pastor. Make some calls, drive around... you know. I'll stay in touch." Olie touched his cap in a brief salute and turned to go, but Grady grabbed his arm.

"Don't I need to sign any papers for a complaint?" he asked.

Olie was surprised. Most things like this were handled "unofficially," with very little in the way of paperwork. "You want to file a complaint, Pastor? But we don't even know if it was them or not. You can't file a complaint without me knowing who to charge."

He released Olie's sleeve. "I guess you're right. But when we do find out, I *will* file a complaint and I *will* press charges." Grady's voice sounded very firm, just like when he condemned drunkenness or lechery from the pulpit.

Officer Olie started the Dodge four-by-four pickup he drove as his wintertime patrol vehicle. Sometimes he needed the extra traction to get through the snow or pull some poor joker from a drift. The local radio station was playing "Grandma Got Run Over By a Reindeer" and Olie smiled. He always thought that one was funny, no matter how many times he heard it. He wiped the smile from his face as he drove by Pastor Snow. It wouldn't do for him to think Olie was laughing at the predicament, although he had to admit it had a humorous side.

Olie stopped by Lynette's Pasties and Coffee for a hot cup of decaf, and the bell over the door tinkled as he entered.

"Mornin', Olie. Same as usual?" Sandra asked him from behind the counter. She was putting fresh pasties and donuts in the display case.

"Yeah, Sandra, and make it a large, double-sugar and double cream. I need the energy this morning."

"You got it." She poured the coffee and handed it to him with the extra packets of sugar. "One double-double." Her eyes looked tired.

"You alright, Sandra?" he asked as he stirred his coffee and blew on the contents of the cup to cool it. "You look like you been up all night long."

She snorted. "'Bout have. Doggone deep fryer broke down yesterday, and the guy didn't get it fixed until almost seven o'clock last night. Then I had to clean it, refill it with grease..." She shook her head. "Anyhow, I couldn't start cooking up today's doughnuts and stuff until almost midnight last night. Was here 'til about 3:30, then went home and crashed."

Olie whistled. "Say, not much sleep! You gonna be OK here?"

She nodded. "Lars is coming around at noon, and he'll spell me while I take a nap. I'll come back around five and help him close up."

Olie stirred his coffee with one of the little wooden sticks Sandra kept in a cup by the register. "Sandra, since you were here so late last night... hmmm. Did you notice any unusual traffic or anything like that?"

Sandra folded her ample arms on the glass case and looked at Olie over her glasses. "Why? What happened?"

"Somebody made off with all the cutout human figures from the crèche at the Lutheran church and..."

Sandra gasped. "The devil you say!" Then she laughed, as though ashamed of doing it. "I bet Reverend Snow is on the warpath right about now, then." She poured herself a cup of coffee as Olie told her the rest of the details.

"You know, I *did* hear something unusual last night, although I didn't see anything. I mean, I was back there," and she jerked a thumb toward the kitchen, "so I didn't see much of anything but grease and flour for a while. But not long before I hauled my tired butt outta here, somebody drove by out front with some mighty loud music playing. Sounded like that that rap junk my nephew listens to—lots of bass thumpin'. Made the windows shake."

"But you didn't see the vehicle?"

"Sorry, no. You think it was the Fantastic Four, or whoever kidnapped the crèche figures?"

Olie shook his head. "I don't know for sure, but sounds like it could've been." He turned toward the door, and then paused. "Oh, Sandra, what's the Pasty of the Day?"

"Chicken-vegetable. You want one?"

"No, I'll drop by for one at lunch, though, if you have any left."

She nodded. "I'll save you one, Olie."

Olie drove through town, making his normal rounds. As one of the only two police officers in Swensen, he had to stay pretty busy checking things out. He waved at a few people, stopped and chatted a little with two more shopkeepers, but nobody had any ideas about who had taken the figures. He stretched the loop he usually drove, to go by his own house. Melanie, may she rest in peace, always wanted him to go by the house and check it a couple of times when she was alive, and he hadn't stopped checking when his wife died four years before.

Olie walked through the house, making the usual cursory inspection, and stuck his head into each room. He almost walked away from Thor's room, but stopped and slowly re-entered it. On the floor were two 12-gauge buckshot shells. Olie drew his brows together, and looked in his son's closet. Normally, his son kept his Remington 870 pump shotgun in the corner of the closet. It wasn't there now.

He considered for a moment, then used his cell to dial his son's workplace. "Andy, Officer Olafsen here. I meant to ask Thor something today but I clean forgot before I left, so I thought I'd give him a call from the office. Can I speak with him? What's that? Oh. Well, he wasn't feeling too good when I left," Olie lied. "Maybe I better drop by the house and check on him. Yeah, thanks, I'll tell him you said that." Olie hung up the phone and stared at the shotgun shells in his hand. Ideas started gelling, and he sure wasn't happy about the form they took.

As Olie backed out of his driveway, he thought about where Thor might be. *The Meadows?* Nah... too many people hunting out there this time of year. *The old landfill?* No, they had just started doing some earthmoving out there for development.

He slapped the steering wheel so hard he hurt his palm. The Hoffers' old place! Matt and Rowena Hoffer both died about two years ago, and their farm was basically abandoned. Oh, their nephew inherited it, but he was too busy over in Minot to come over very often, so it just sat there and went to weed most of the time. He once caught Mike Pearce parking out there with Brenda Peterson, too. Olie turned right at the next street and made his way to County Road K.

The road to the old Hoffer place was rutted and the stiff shocks in the Dodge didn't have much resilience, so Olie lost half of his coffee to spillage on the way. As he approached the turn-in for the old farm, he heard the echoing "boom!" of a shotgun. A grim look crossed his face. *Maybe it'll be hunters*, he thought, *but I doubt it.*

He parked the big Dodge Ram pickup across the driveway entrance to keep anyone from getting out or in while he was there, and started up the driveway on foot. As he started on his way, an uneasy idea came to him and he returned to the truck to fetch his own shotgun, a short-barreled riot gun. He didn't figure he'd need it, but it never hurt to have something more than a badge to show for authority.

He heard another shotgun blast, and then one more. He heard the faint sound of laughter as he walked up the side of the road, keeping to the cover of the young pines growing there. When he came to a curve in the road, he peered through the branches and saw three vehicles: Mike Pearce's pickup, Wesley Hansen's old Plymouth and his son Thor's twenty-year-old Jeep. Olie pressed his lips together in a tight line. *Melanie, I'm sorry. I thought I taught him what to do and what not to do. I'll do better, I promise.*

He stepped back behind the cover of the pine saplings and used his mobile phone. "Pastor Snow? I think I've found your crèche figures. I'm out at the old Hoffer place, where I can see Mike Pearce's truck and Wesley Hansen's car. I think they're shooting at the figures with shotguns…" He heard an outraged squawk through the phone. "Don't worry, maybe we can salvage them. I'm going to try to talk to them now." He closed the connection with the minister still exploding with outrage at the other end of the line.

Olie checked to be sure he had a round in the chamber of his own shotgun, and eased himself out of hiding. Following the fenceline, he made his way around to where he could clearly see the east side of the barn. Sure enough, there were the Fantastic Four, and Thor, all standing with shotguns in their hands and laughing. Three of the figures had already been blasted, it was obvious: one of the three magi was missing a head, and there were gaping, splintered holes in the figure of Joseph and another of the magi. Wesley walked forward, and moved the plywood cutout of another wise man, leaning it against the barn wall where they were shooting. Holes from the shotgun blasts peppered the old oaken boards.

"This 'un's yours, Thor! See what you can do to that wise man, there!" Mike was egging him on. "See if you can take off his head like I did to the first 'un!"

Olie was walking toward the boys now, and as Wesley turned around from putting the second of the magi into place, he caught sight of the constable and froze in place.

"Come on, Wesley, get outta th' way! Thor's gotta shoot that old geezer!" Mike yelled, but Wesley just shook his head and gestured. As the other boys followed his pointing finger, Olie fired one round from his riot shotgun into the air, and all the boys jumped.

"Put the guns down on the ground, fellas," Olie ordered them as he racked in a fresh round. "I know you wouldn't shoot me on purpose, but we gotta make sure no accidents happen." All the boys but one complied immediately, their guns clattering on the hard ground. Thor hesitated, his eyes locked on his father's. "That includes you, Thor Olafsen," the constable said in a commanding tone, with a touch of sadness that he couldn't banish. Blinking, Thor bent and placed his shotgun on the ground as well.

"Now, all of you go over and lean up against Mike's truck, facing it. Put your hands on the backs of your heads."

"Aw, Olie, come on now! We wasn't…"

"Shut up right now, Billy Anderson, before you make me madder than I already am. There's a lot going on here. Theft… from a *church*, for goodness sake! Vandalism. Trespassing. Destruction of property. Use of firearms in commission of a crime." Olie was irate, and let it show. "And Pastor Snow has already said he's going to press charges. I called him before I showed myself to you boys."

The boys' faces looked stricken, and Thor looked especially pale. "Dad, I'm sorry. I didn't…."

"Get over against the truck, like I said, all of you, and just shut up. Save it for your defense." The boys moved to comply with the constable's order, and Olie placed a set of plastic zip-tie handcuffs on each one. He checked their pockets and removed the inevitable folding hunting knife from each boy's belt or pocket, placing them all on the seat of the pickup. He pulled all five boys around in front of himself.

"OK, now move. We're walking out to my truck, which is parked across the driveway to this place." He prodded them all with the butt of his shotgun, even Thor, and they stumbled on down the drive, toward the road. He was wondering how he was going to get them all in the club cab of his pickup, but he knew he couldn't put any of them in the back, even with the camper shell.

When he arrived at the parked Dodge pickup, he saw another vehicle there: Pastor Snow had driven out and was parked beside his truck. The middle-aged man was obviously angry, but as he watched the five boys' dejected progress toward him, his face softened a little.

"I'm glad you're here," Olie called to him. "I couldn't get all these miscreants into my truck. Will you help me take them back to the county administration building?"

Two of the boys got into the back of Olie's club cab pickup, but his son was not one of them. Thor rode with the minister, along with Mike and Wesley.

***

The next morning, Officer Olafsen dropped by Pastor Snow's home to visit. "Do you still intend to press charges, Pastor? You have the right, but… is it the best thing?"

Pastor Snow sat, drumming his fingers on the dining room table as he contemplated the question. "I have to pray about this, Olie," he finally said. "I have to seek counsel from Above."

***

That evening, the colored floodlights came on at 6:00 PM sharp, as Perry Como crooned "Do You Hear What I Hear?" over the amplified speakers. The crèche was complete. Olie dropped by once more and stood beside Pastor Snow as they watched the procession of gawkers photographing the Christmas scene.

"It looks very nice, Pastor. Very realistic."

Pastor Snow sighed. "Yes, very nice indeed. I think the extra publicity from the theft actually increased the number of people driving by, too. Providence can bring good out of evil, as I've always said." Olie almost strangled on his coffee, but said nothing.

One of the three wise men (Melchior, Olie believed) reached up and scratched his nose, then sneezed. Joseph adjusted his position on the ground beside the manger.

"The boys are going to make new plywood figures, too, right?"

The minister nodded. "Yes, and the Ladies Auxiliary will decorate them as they did before."

Olie sipped some more coffee. Good stuff. The pastor's wife knew how to make good coffee, even if she wasn't much at knitting. A skinny Christmas tree that leaned to the left adorned the pastor's sweater this time.

The pastor continued, "And they all signed the agreement to be living crèche figures for three hours every night, through the end of December." He looked up at Olie. "Once you told them what they *could* be charged with, they found it to be a pretty good deal."

Olie put his coffee mug down. "You did the right thing, Reverend. Pressing charges would be pretty destructive to all their lives, but maybe they'll learn something from it this way."

"I... I'm sorry that your son has to be out there, too, Olie. He really didn't shoot at any of the figures, and he wasn't involved in the actual theft. They all agreed that was true, so..."

Olie interrupted him. "It's a good lesson for Thor, Reverend Snow. I doubt he'll ever forget it." He looked at his watch. "And I need to be going. I have to make the rounds, you know."

As Olie drove around the little town that night, checking on storefronts, he talked to Melanie again. He did it pretty often, though he wouldn't have admitted it. *I hope you aren't mad at me for making the suggestion to Pastor Snow about the crèche figures. I figured it was better than Thor having a record or going to jail.* He listened for a moment, but didn't hear or feel any disapproval.

Olie reached over and punched the power button on the radio. Once more, "Grandma Got Run Over By A Reindeer" was playing, and Olie smiled as he hummed along.

Copyright ©2007, Tony Burton

Ballet Exercises
Gay Toltl Kinman

Celeste did her cool-down exercises after the ballet class, dressed, quickly pulled on her cowboy boots and rushed to her car.

She'd make it in time for her night class in economics if there wasn't a delay on the freeway. With one hand, she rummaged around in her voluminous shoulder bag through books and the other paraphernalia of her life, searching for an energy bar she knew would probably be squashed beyond recognition by now.

She pushed the radio on. Tinny Christmas jingles followed by, "Only three more days of shopping days before Christmas. And now for the news. Police report finding the body of an unidentified woman who according to a Department's spokesperson had been knifed and raped..." Celeste pushed the button off.

I don't want to hear that, too depressing, she thought. She'd have to wait until the news was over to get any music, even it was just Jingle Bells and White Christmas interspersed with shopping commercials. She had no one to buy for, so it didn't matter how many days were left.

The traffic was hopeless, everyone was going somewhere. Sunday was Christmas. Her last class, then two weeks of vacation.

Eventually, she was able to get music, but only Christmas songs that sounded dissonant, jarring as though on a worn tape.

The parking lot at the community college

was almost empty. Her class must be the only one in session, or else everyone had cut. The buildings looked deserted. She shivered in the brisk, bone-chilling wind blowing through the Coyote Canyon as she ran in. No time to go to the ladies room.

The instructor hadn't arrived and only half the class was there. After ten minutes he was still a no-show. The murmurings about leaving became louder. Then someone cited the heavy traffic, so they waited another five minutes before dashing off to their real lives.

Celeste ran to the ladies room. One of the double doors, the outie, was propped open. She ran in.

While she was in the stall she heard the door slam shut. She came out doing up her belt.

Santa Claus was standing by the sinks.

Janitor? Someone in the wrong rest room?

He was smirking. Fear gripped her.

"You don't have to bother buttonin' up, darlin', cause I'm going to be takin' 'em right down again."

Her mind splintered.

Cell phone? In the car.

Gun? Home in the nightstand.

He advanced—like a man who was going to get what he wanted.

She could hardly breathe.

When he was closer, Celeste swung her heavy leather bag with every ballet muscle she'd ever exercised, and connected. The large metal clasp caught him on the side of his head. He staggered and went down on one knee. She ran past him and pushed on the exit door that had been open.

Locked.

She threw herself against the other one, but she knew it only opened in and there was no handle on it. She scrabbled at the bottom but there was no space for her fingers to get under to pull it open.

Celeste pushed against the outie door again. It still didn't budge. She banged on it with her fists, screaming, "Help, help!"

Who would be left to hear her?

He had probably waited until everyone was gone.

Suddenly, there was a grip on her shoulder. His hand.

She whirled out of his grasp.

His mouth was open—she could see his rotten teeth. He held up the key like a trophy.

The bastard had locked them in.

She had to get the key.

"You're goin' to pay for that." His eyes were so demented that she froze. He lurched toward her.

In her head she heard her ballet teacher, *"One, two, three, jette!"*

She did, catching him not quite in the groin of his red pants, but enough to throw him off balance again. Not enough for him to drop the key.

He pulled something out of his pocket. She heard a click and saw the knife sparkling in the light.

How could she defend herself?

Mace.

She had a can of Mace.

Somewhere in the rat's nest of her purse.

"Looks like I'm going to be cuttin' you."

The newscast—the woman the police found, knifed and raped. Unidentified.

He came closer.

Jette!

This time she connected as he sliced down through the leather of her boot to her leg.

The knife flew to the left as he bent over in pain. She kicked again, catching his jaw. He flew back his head clunking on a sink. He slid to the floor. Immobile

The key went under the sinks to the right.

Key or knife?

Key.

She grabbed it up, her nails rasping against the cement floor, ran to the door, tried to unlock it. Her hand was shaking so much she could hardly get the key in the lock but she did.

And turned it—just as she was pulled to the floor, falling hard, the contents of her bag spilling.

He gripped her booted leg, dragged her toward him.

She twisted, then kicked him hard in the face with the heel of her other boot. She heard a crack and his nose bled but he still clung to her leg. His body odor choked her.

As she tried to brace herself to pull away, her hand touched one of the contents of her purse—the Mace.

She grasped it, fumbling with the case.

He lunged up at her, climbing up over her boots. She held her breath and closed her eyes and sprayed him with a short burst. Like she was spraying a cockroach.

He screamed, crawling to the sink, splashing his eyes with water. She scooped everything into her bag, held the Mace like a gun and turned the key in the lock. She sprayed the Mace at him as she backed out of the door and locked it once more.

She was tearing, shaking so badly she could hardly stand. She grabbed the doorframe. Her hand fell on the light switch. She flipped it down. The lights in the ladies room went off.

She lurched to the end of the hallway and pulled the door open gasping the fresh, cold air of freedom.

She reached into her jeans pocket for her car keys, then dropped them twice before she could unlock the car. And twice more before she got the key into the ignition. The radio came on.

Her teeth chattered and her body shook. She turned the heat to high.

As she opened the glovebox for her cell phone, the newscaster said "Police have identified the body of the woman who had been knifed and raped..."

She stretched a shaking hand to the phone.

That could have been her.

It almost *was* her.

She could have been his next victim. Now she was mad. He'd dared mess with her. He'd dared to try to rape her, cut her.

What if she called and the police came and he never got convicted? Even with what she told them about what happened? What if she went though the trial and all of that? And he was let off. She knew it could happen.

He would try again. To get even. He know where to find her after the trial. He'd have her address.

He could come for her. She wouldn't be able to get away as she had tonight. He wouldn't let her. It'd be worse. He'd torture her to get even.

Her left hand cradled the phone as a right finger hovered over the buttons.

9-1-1?

What if she waited for a few days? He'll be locked in there until then, hungry, desperate and in pain. Like his victims. What if she waited until after Christmas? Maybe even after the winter break?

She could leave him there.

She leaned sideways to put the phone back.

The compartment's light shone on it like a spotlight.

Her gun.

It wasn't in her nightstand. She had put it in the glove compartment—she remembered now.

She still had the key to the ladies room door.

What if she went back?

With her gun.

Copyright ©2005 Gay Toltl Kinman

Christmas Every Day
Margaret Fenton

The rack in front of her shined with glossy covers featuring decadent holiday foods, and she faked interest in one of them while keeping an eye on the dark-haired woman in line just ahead of her. Reaching, she picked up one of the magazines. <u>Our Best Christmas Recipes Ever,</u> said the cover. She pretended to study one for fruitcake. The teenaged clerk scanned can after can from the black conveyor and whistled "Jingle Bell Rock" softly along with the piped-in music. Then, finally, "One hundred and sixty one oh seven. Ma'am," he added as an afterthought.

This was it. The timing was crucial. The woman opened her wallet, took out her debit card and swiped it through the scanner. She watched carefully as the woman typed in the four numbers. 5797. Now.

She moved to replace the magazine, her elbow knocking over the plastic jug of grape juice whose lid she'd surreptitiously loosened minutes earlier. It fell off the belt, hit the floor, and bounced, splashing purple liquid all over both the women's shoes and everything else within a three foot radius.

"Oh, *hell*," she said. "I'm so sorry."
The woman shot her a look. "It's okay."
"No really, I'm so sorry."
The teenager reached below the counter

and came up with a roll of paper towels. He jogged around to their side and in the sticky chaos as they mopped up their legs and feet and the floor, no one noticed her hand slipping into the woman's open purse and sliding the wallet into her jacket pocket.

It was just that easy.

In her car, blocks away, she opened the wallet. *Who am I today?* she thought, reading the driver's license. *Ah, I'm Susan Ambrose. Five feet seven, black hair, brown eyes. Easy enough.* She pulled over onto a quiet residential street, quickly trading the blond wig for a black one. The juice-stained heels she traded for flats. The dark glasses would hide her eyes, and the fur-lined hood of her coat would take care of the rest. She checked the mirror on the back of the sun flap and sped to the nearest bank.

She knew a hundred ways of getting other people's money. She'd dabbled in phishing, getting personal information by sending out realistic-looking emails as if they'd come from a bank. Too many people were on to that scam now. Fake shopping websites were lucrative, but with a catch. Too easy to track. Raiding mailboxes for pre-approved credit card upgrade letters was a good one, especially this time of year when it seemed everyone went into debt for the holidays. All you had to do was scribble a signature on the application form and watch the box for the card. Then a little caller ID spoofing, and presto, a new line of credit.

Of course, getting debit or credit cards by stealing them directly was the best way, but the riskiest. She only had a limited amount of time before the real Susan Ambrose would notice her wallet was gone, traipse back to the store, find she hadn't left it there, and start calling the bank. Any transactions had to be done immediately. First she'd get the cash, withdrawing the limit from the ATM. Then, shopping.

Eventually she found a parking space and joined the massive crowd as they strolled up and down the mall, under the giant holly wreaths, peeking into festive shop windows, pointing and wanting. The excitement was in the air, for sure. It meant nothing to her. She passed a long line of cranky mothers and children waiting to have a snapshot and a moment with Santa. She had no children and wished she could forget her childhood. She wasn't religious, so the whole reason-for-the-season thing didn't appeal. And presents? Well, she had those. Christmas every day. Just without the wrapping paper and the tree. All she needed was a series of sixteen numbers on a little plastic card.

She ducked into a store and bought an exquisite dress before continuing her errand. She'd picked out her next purchase yesterday at a boutique store, the cute red bikini with the matching cover-up. She may not celebrate Christmas, but red was the color of the season.

She'd had a heck of a time finding a bathing suit this time of the year. And it was expensive, but wasn't that the point? Once that was bought, plus one or two other items, she'd ditch the Ambrose woman's cards in a dumpster, retrieve the rest of her saved cash from her apartment, find a travel agency she hadn't used before and buy the ticket.

A mere five days later the shoreline of Fort Lauderdale was a distant line on the horizon. In two days they'd be in Colon, Panama, then on to Costa Rica, and finally Belize. Her cabin was lovely, the balcony a nice place to sit and enjoy coffee in the mornings. Her steward, a handsome Jamaican boy named James, saw to her every need. The entire staff of the ship was wearing cheap fuzzy Santa hats along with their brightly printed uniforms, but she supposed that couldn't be helped. It was impossible to escape the Christmas madness entirely.

The air was still a bit chilly at this time of the afternoon, so she opted to skip the bikini for now and donned a short blue tropical-patterned dress and her big floppy hat. Sunglasses on, she found an empty chaise on the Lido deck and was browsing the December Elle magazine when the pages fell into shadow.

"Anyone sitting here?" asked a man's voice.

"No."

He threw one leg over the chair and

sank into it. "Thanks. You cruising with your family?"

"No." She really wasn't in the mood for small talk and pointedly stared at the Gucci ad in her lap.

"Me neither. Course, I don't have much of a family, now that I'm divorced. My ex took the kids with her. She didn't get all the money, though, thank God. I've got a great financial planner who really knows what he's doing."

She folded down the corner of the page and turned to him for the first time. Navy board shorts. He was really too old for board shorts, he was in his fifties at least, and the orange and white Hawaiian shirt he was wearing was totally garish. The body, already slightly burned from the sun, wasn't bad at all, but his haircut needed updating. She suspected he'd worn it the same way since 1984. What he needed, she realized, was a woman. A woman with taste.

"That's a good friend to have," she answered, throwing him a flirtatious smile.

"You betcha. Where you from?"

"New York," she lied.

"This your first cruise?"

"Oh, no. I'm a travel writer. Freelance. For magazines and such. I'm working on an article about holiday cruises." It was amazing, really, how easily the lies came. As if they were all buried somewhere in her head, just waiting to be told.

"That's a great job. You're lucky."

"Most of the time. Except when the work's a little thin. What about you?"

"I'm a lawyer. Contracts. Nothing very exciting, and very little travel. This year, after the divorce and all, Christmas was going to be tough. I just had to get away. Away from the ice and snow and all the holiday hassle, you know?"

"I know. I despise Christmas. All of it, from the fake good cheer to the plastic Santas. Anything phony really bothers me." She covered a smile.

"You know," he said, "there should be a club for people like us. People who hate Christmas. Like an Anti-Christmas Club."

"True. We could be the charter members."

He held out a hand. "Put her there, partner. What's your name?"

She shook his hand, letting her fingers rest a little longer than necessary in his palm. She gave him the name she was traveling under, the most exotic of her repertoire. "Marissa. Marissa Almada."

"That's beautiful."

"Thank you. It's Spanish." She had no idea if it was or not, but she looked the part of the Spanish beauty. Her hair was dyed deep chestnut brown, accentuated by a dark spray tan.

"I'm Jack. Jack Rodgers."

"Pleased to meet you, Jack."

"By the way, what anti-Christmas activities do you have planned for tonight?"

She agreed to dine with him the first night, and they met by the pool the next day. She caught his appreciative looks at her red swimsuit, allowed him to rub her back with suntan lotion. Their conversation, mostly meaningless chat, occasionally focused on her made-up job, her made-up apartment, or her made-up family. It was all so easy and fun.

And she genuinely liked Jack. His smile was always just underneath the surface, as if he were always enjoying himself. He listened patiently to her stories, asked her questions about her interests, even though they weren't real. She found herself, over the course of the two days they spent together—and for the first time in a long time—feeling a little guilty. What if he was the one? The one who would allow her to give it all up. No more seducing, no more sneaking. He could be her Prince Charming and Santa Claus, all rolled into one. As long as he had money, and it seemed he did. He'd dropped little hints all day: the Mustang he bought "just for fun," the condo on the shore his wife hadn't gotten in the settlement, and so forth.

On the last night before landing in Colon, she met him in the dining room for the second seating. She'd dressed with him in mind, choosing a black haltered Ralph Lauren that highlighted her thin shoulders. Her hair she arranged elegantly in an up-do so to show off the diamond earrings. She spotted Jack from the door, saw his gaze sweep her body slowly as he waved her over to the table.

One of the tuxedoed waiters held her chair for her, placed her napkin in her lap. A miniature Christmas tree graced the middle of the white-clothed table, peppermint candy ornaments on the branches. "Hi," she said to Jack with a smile.

"Hi. Gorgeous dress."

"Thanks." She looked down at the small plate in front of her and saw the package for the first time. It was square, flat, and wrapped in blue paper with tiny reindeer on it.

"Jack," she said, a remonstrative tone to her voice. "What's this? I told you I don't celebrate—."

"I know. Neither do I. It's just a little something I thought would look good on you. Go ahead, open it."

She smiled at him. "Okay. Just this once, though. And I have to buy you something in town tomorrow."

"Deal."

She peeled off the paper carefully. It was a necklace box, the black velvet delicious in her hands. She cracked it open slowly, saw a glimpse of something silver...

Before she could even think, react, anything, Jack snapped the bracelets on her wrists with a click.

"Merry Christmas. You're under arrest." The ship rolled, like they'd hit a big wave.

"You're a cop? But I was so careful—" Shut up, a voice in her head screamed. Not one more word until you get a lawyer. One of the waiters grabbed her arm and was holding it tightly.

"Special Agent Jack Rogers at your service. Susan Morgan Ambrose, you are charged with the murder of your husband, Donald Ambrose. Anything you say…"

Wait a minute. "What? I'm charged with what?"

"You are charged with the murder of your husband, Donald. Did you really think we wouldn't find the body?"

"Body? What body?" Who the hell was Susan Ambrose?

"Very clever, dumping his body in the lake, telling all your friends and family you'd both be on vacation until after the New Year. But he's been suspecting something like this would happen for months, ever since you starting moving his money into foreign banks. Just couldn't stand being cut out of the will, could you? And that's exactly what would have happened once the divorce was final."

Susan Ambrose, which one was Susan Ambrose? She scrolled through memories in her mind, names, faces, driver's licenses, passports…

The woman from the grocery store. The wallet she'd boosted in the checkout line. She saw it clearly in her mind now, right down to what the woman had been buying. Canned goods, bottled water, and over the counter drugs, lots of them. And hair dye. Boxes and boxes of hair dye.

She of all people should have seen it. Those were the groceries of someone going into hiding.

And the real Mrs. Ambrose would never reappear now. Not when someone else had been arrested for her crime.

Jack continued. "We've been watching you. Watching you pull money out of his accounts. Watching all the expensive shopping trips. Too bad we couldn't get to you before you killed him. And I have to say, *Marissa*, that's some disguise you pulled off. Got your backstory all worked out, too, didn't you? Travel writer, holiday cruises, New York. Never had any intention of getting back on the boat in Panama, did you? Nice try."

The truth. The truth was all she had. "But I'm not Susan Ambrose."

"Uh huh."

"Really! I'm not! My real name is..." God, what was it? She hadn't used it in so long she had to think about it.

"Save it," Jack said. "Save it for the judge."

Copyright ©2007 Margaret Fenton

Have a Harpy Christmas
by Peggy Jaegly

Her hands and ankles were trussed and her mouth stuffed like a Christmas turkey. A piece of duct tape sealed her lips. Rebecca had to fight the urge to gag and tried to calm the hopelessness rising in her chest. She wiggled her wrists, bound behind her back, attempting to loosen the rope. The kidnappers abandoned her when they heard the auditorium door open and slam shut. Catching sight of a nail sticking out of a backstage stud, she pressed down on her feet and her hands and scooted herself to the wall. She groaned with effort and dismay as her performance gown collected years of dust, typical of most dark backstage floors. She shouldn't have stayed alone in the theatre after the dress rehearsal. Panic at performing on stage in front of 1,000 people tomorrow drove her to double her practice time.

She reached the nail and carefully pressed her cheek to it. Catching the edge of the tape, she tried to loosen one corner. It was in this awkward position, looking like she was kissing the wall, that Manny found her. Her agent, a handsome dark Italian, was short and stocky, but packed a bundle of energy in everything he did. His success in the entertainment industry was due to his intelligence and his never-failing positive disposition.

"Becky! What happened?" He removed the duct tape as gently as he could. The residue left her face feeling raw and sticky. Her eyes watered as her tongue moved to moisten her mouth. She felt vomit rising, but took a moment to breathe deeply through her nose. All those Zen books Manny had lent her to get over her stage fright were working.

As soon as she could, she croaked, "Two men with hoods grabbed me when I came backstage." She coughed from the proximity of the dust, an allergen of hers.

Manny untied her wrists. "Your hands? How are your hands?" He held them to examine. "You've got to play for the Toys for Tots gala tomorrow night."

Rebecca pulled her fingers to palm. Two of the calluses were bleeding. "My wrists are bruised but the fingers still work."

He rubbed her fingertips. "You've got to stop practicing so much. Save it for tomorrow."

"It's your fault for scheduling me for a stage event. How many times do I have to tell you, I like playing background music, not front and center?" As her agent, Manny never listened to her. She loved playing the harp, mostly for patients in the hospital. Manny kept pushing her to play for bigger and bigger venues, despite her reluctance due to stage fright. It was he who stocked her condo with Zen meditation and yoga books and instructional audios.

"I know. I know. But can I help it if you're in demand?"

Rebecca silently knew he was right but refused to admit it to him. Her career had catapulted since he became her agent six months ago. She wanted to stay in the background, do the simple gigs. Manny pretended to listen, then ignored her pleas and booked her for highly visible performances. Money had never flowed so freely, especially from her CD sales. If she didn't put her foot down, he'd probably start scheduling television appearances.

"Let me help you up," Manny said, after releasing the rope knot around her feet. "Are you all right?"

"As good as I can be under the circumstances." Rebecca brushed at her gown. "What did those men want?"

"Um… I can guess."

"Man-n-n-y?" she elongated his name. "What have you not been telling me now?" Her agent had a penchant for eliminating details that he thought might upset her. He claimed ownership to handling problems so she could concentrate on composing music. It rubbed against her independent woman grain. In fact, lots of Manny's habits irritated her. In many ways they were opposites. Reluctantly, she concluded, that's probably why they worked well as a team.

"They were probably recording your harp music."

"My practicing?"

"Hey, your practicing is better than other's performances."

"Why in the world?" Rebecca couldn't imagine.

"Tony called me today. There was a break in at the studio."

"Was anyone hurt?" Rebecca placed a hand over her heart in shock. She abhorred hearing or reading about people injured or worse and hoped her favorite engineer was fine.

"It happened last night. Whoever broke in ransacked his place. He doesn't know yet if anything is missing. Uh…"

"Manny, tell me everything!"

"He won't know for certain until he restores order but…" Manny hesitated. Rebecca could visualize his mind whirring to sugarcoat the truth.

"Everything," her mouth formed a grim line.

"The master of your new CD *might* be missing."

"But the CDs are already made for tonight's benefit sale."

"Unless the thieves want to sell pirated copies," Manny reminded her. Rebecca never expected the true nature of less than scrupulous people. *Good thing she has me to protect her.*

"But all those profits are earmarked for charity." Donating to those in need had always been paramount to Rebecca, even before she was wealthy. She'd grown up without much and didn't want others to needlessly suffer. "So not only us, but all those kids are being robbed too."

She paced the stage to her harp, released the pedal tensions and covered it. Slinging her gig bag over her shoulder, she turned to Manny. "We need to call the police."

"Definitely." Manny helped her transport her harp off stage and secured it in a locked room. "I'll see what my people can find out."

Rebecca shook her head. She liked following the rules, and Manny liked bending them. "Just because we *accidentally* figured who attacked the bishop a few months ago, doesn't make us detectives. Let the police do their job." Rebecca didn't know much about Manny's background. His credentials were impressive but sometimes she wondered about his associations. He did get results, she admitted to herself grudgingly.

"My connections can get information cops can't and without ruffling the wrong feathers."

"I thought any publicity was good publicity."

"You don't want to ruin a kids Christmas party, do you?" Manny appealed to her philanthropic gene.

"I give up!" Rebecca threw up her hands and made her way to the exit.

Manny followed her. "My car's out front. I'm dropping you off. You're a star and I'll make sure nothing else bad happens to you tonight."

"The thugs were kidnapping me. They only left me when they heard you call my name." She smiled at him. "By the way, I forgot to say thank you!" Alarm started in her stomach and rose through her body like an overheated thermometer. Her nerves were on edge about tomorrow's event; she didn't need the added worry of a repeat appearance of the hooded duo.

"They're not going to get a chance to get close to you," Manny said. "I'll see to that." He eased his Jaguar onto the freeway. "To be on the safe side, we're beefing up security and no more solo practices. You hear?"

Rebecca held her silence as she considered her options.

"Becky, I mean it!"

"Oh, fine." Rebecca relented, then sensed an opportunity. "This is a good reason to stop booking me for stage events."

"Right, babe. You got it."

Rebecca didn't believe him.

Manny continued, intent on changing the subject. "Did you see anything that would help identify the cretins?"

She thought a moment. "Shoes. I noticed the shoes of the one who tied me up." She closed her eyes, willing herself to remember details. "They were dark and thick soled. Work boots. Like the kind my dad wore in construction."

"Anything else?"

"He wore jeans. They covered any logo on the shoes, but there was a scuff mark on the right shoe—like something had torn across the front."

"That's a start." Manny pulled into her parking spot and helped her to the door. He insisted on a quick tour of her place to rule out hidden lurkers. "Unfortunately, it could be someone very close to us," he warned her. "One of the engineers or photographers at the studio."

"And they all wear jeans," Rebecca agreed.

She offered him a decaf coffee while they mulled over who would have a motive.

"Steve, who handles the lights, looks like he could use the money," Manny mused. "Scruffy hair, tattoos all over the place."

"I don't think so. Steve and I just discussed the latest best seller novel. Do you know he reads 100 books a year?"

"Then he's got the brains to finesse a plot."

"Manny, I don't want to do this. I don't want to be looking at everyone around me and wonder if they are a criminal. Let's notify the police."

"I'll take care of everything. That's what I'm here for babe. But if I call them now, you won't get a wink of rest. My people are on it. I'll file a report on my way home and hire some off-duties for tomorrow. You," Manny rose and placed his mug on the coffee table, "get to bed. Call me when you're ready to go tomorrow. I'm escorting you to the gala. I'm not letting you out of my sight."

They agreed upon a time and Manny kissed her on the cheek at the door. "Lock it tight!" he ordered her.

Rebecca couldn't bear the thought that someone she worked with could do this. She lit some candles around the tub and soon immersed herself in bubbles to soak the day's tensions away.

The next day, they arrived early to the theatre, hours before she'd go on stage. Rebecca checked on her harp and tuned it. After running through her program once, Manny ordered her out of the room and locked it, stowing the key in his pocket. He knew her well. Left to her own devices, fear would lead her to practice all day.

Tonight, besides being a benefit for Toys for Tots, also marked the debut of her latest CD. It was her best work yet. The CD featured original harp compositions. All the profits were being donated to the cause.

Manny went to check on the boxes of CDs shipped for back-of-the-room sales tonight. Her stomach churned the closer the clock ticked towards evening. She decided to take a walk. Maybe the fresh air would help calm her nerves. She wrapped herself in her overcoat. Her classically cut wool slacks and a turtleneck should keep her warm enough for a walk. She pulled on gloves to protect her hands and sunglasses against the bright sun before exiting the theatre.

She strolled along Main Street inhaling the crisp, winter air. She wandered, taking in the festive lights and the holiday scenes depicted in the department store window displays. The city was celebrating First Friday and many of the stores had sidewalk sales. She meandered among the tables of ornaments, watches, scarves, and jewelry.

One barker called to her, "Pretty Lady. Come see. We've got the best deals." A small group of passersby, cloaked in a colorful mixture of winter jackets, scarves and hats, milled with interest around his table of CDs. Rebecca loved music in all genres and joined the crowd. "Good deals here," the salesman proclaimed to her. "One CD for $5 or three for $12." He flashed a wide smile at her. "Best deal in town!"

Rebecca looked through his selection until she saw her newest CD, lying on the table. Her stomach lurched and her head felt woozy. *How could this be? It wasn't being released until tonight.* The vendor noticed her interest and began his spiel to reel her in.

"You like harp music? She's the best."

    Fearing she'd be recognized, she shoved a five dollar bill in the man's hands and fled with the CD. She ran back to the theatre and searched for Manny. She was breathless when she found him. She shoved the CD in his hands. "I just bought this on the street."

    Manny grabbed his tote with his laptop. They found a janitorial closet with a plug. They listened to the pirated CD. The songs were hers, but the quality poor. They looked at each other and groaned at the scratchy and popcorn sounding audio track.

    Using his cell phone, Manny called the police and gave them the location Rebecca provided. One hour before the performance, an officer reported back to Manny. The vendor was gone by the time the officers arrived. Manny explained the situation to the officer who promised to look into it further. His first stop would be the studio where Rebecca recorded her CD over the course of a month.

    "But the damage is done," Rebecca said.

    "Don't worry about it," her agent assured her. "We'll have you set up to autograph the CDs after your performance. People will want the real thing for what they are paying per plate."

    "Oh, Manny." Rebecca dropped her face into her hands. "I feel sick."

    "Do your breathing exercises. Breathe in 2,3,4, and out, 2,3,4. You can do this."

    "I hate you right now."

"I love you too, babe."

Manny unlocked the room and reunited her with her harp. She checked each string determining each was perfectly tuned. She had just finished when the director called a mandatory meeting for all performers, sound and light engineers in the green room. Distracted, she hardly heard what the director instructed. Manny stood close by and reached out to massage her tight shoulder muscles. She couldn't help but study everyone's shoes.

The meeting concluded and everyone retreated to their assigned places. Backstage, she paced and shook her arms and hands trying to calm herself, the closer it came time for her performance. Her body shuddered as she passed the spot where she had been strung tight last night. Manny, always the bright go-getter, kept repeating positive affirmations to shore up her nerves. "You're great! Concentrate on the music you love. You won't even be able to see anyone from the stage. Pretend you're alone."

His cell phone buzzed. For once, Rebecca was grateful for the interruption.

"Thanks for getting back to me, Tony." He snapped his cell phone shut and grinned at Rebecca.

"That was Tony." He said there may be an embedded ID code on the fake CD. It possibly could reveal what machine copied your CD."

Rebecca felt a small measure of hope.

She didn't have time to enjoy it as the backstage coordinator signaled her to take the stage.

"Break a leg, Becky!" Manny smiled and patted her back. *No need to tell her now, what else Tony had told him. The ID code wouldn't be able to tell them the location of the duplicating machine. No sense in worrying her with details.*

Half an hour later, Rebecca took her bow to thunderous applause. She didn't know how she got through it. Harp music always soothed her whether she was playing or listening to it. She didn't even remember playing half the songs, but here she was, done. *What a relief!*

Manny was ecstatic. "Roland came backstage to tell me how much he enjoyed your performance," he told her. "He says 'you're smashing!'" *I'll tell her later how the English producer wants to book her to perform on stage in England.*

Rebecca's body felt limp with relief and damp from the burning stage lights. Stage hands transported her harp off stage. As her body drained of tension, an idea occurred to her. "Manny, you're busy right now, but while I'm waiting for the autograph session, I want to listen to the pirated CD again. After getting the keys from Manny, she followed her harp to its secure room. She closed the door behind the stage hands and inserted the CD into Manny's laptop, turning the volume down low so only she could hear it. While the counterfeit tracks played, she studied the printed CD case with its list of songs. If her hunch was right, it could narrow down the list of possible suspects.

She remembered that two different master cuts had been made. The recording studio always kept a disc of the final recording and she received two. One master disc was sent to the replicating company, the studio and she each kept one for safe keeping. Manny hadn't been with her for the last session when she picked up the masters. She didn't like the mix and Tony quickly adjusted the reverb and cut her a new master. At the last minute, she also had him eliminate one of the songs that didn't meet her standards when she heard the final track. If *Snowy Sunday* was on this CD, then it could be only one of three people from the studio who would have had access to it: Tony and Rick, both the studio owners and engineers, or Lowell, their part-time assistant. Tony had broken and discarded the first master she didn't like. Even she didn't have a copy of the rejected master, since Tony remastered the final one immediately. The title was omitted on the artwork for the CD cover and back label. Somehow Rebecca figured bootleggers wouldn't be diligent enough to compare a pirated disc with the text on the back of the CD. They were money, not music lovers.

Midway through the disc, she cringed as

the refrain for *Snowy Sunday* played. She thought of the three men in the studio. Tony and she had worked together for years. A practicing Christian and Sunday school teacher, she doubted he would be the culprit. Hadn't he even provided Manny a clue to seek out the duplicating machine? She also deduced that Rick, his partner, had very little to gain for illegally copying her CD. Neither Tony nor Rick would want poor quality CDs on the market with their sound studio name as a credit on the label. That left Lowell. She stopped the CD and snapped the computer off. She had to tell Manny.

Rebecca jumped as the door to the room creaked open. "Manny, I was just …." she stopped. The shoe with the scuff mark stepped into the room. Her eyes took in the jeans and traveled up to the face. She gulped. "Hi Lowell!" She hoped her enthusiasm didn't sound too fake. "Did you come to the show?"

"Yeah, right." He entered the room and pressed his back against the door to close it. "One ticket is half the cost of the guitar I want."

The click of the doorjamb triggered alarm bells in Rebecca's head. She stood and placed the cover over her harp and pretended to just notice her watch. "Oh, look at the time. I have to get to the autograph table or Manny will go ballistic."

Lowell, shuffled and stammered, "Uh, do you have a cell phone? I need to call my mom for a ride home."

Maybe she was wrong. After all he was a gangly teenager, just 17 years old, and he seemed timid enough. "Sure. She dug into her gig bag and retrieved it. As a precaution, she slipped one of her spare wire strings and a pair of wire cutters into her pocket with the hand out of Lowell's view. She proffered the phone to Lowell. "I'm sure Manny would offer you a ride home, but we have a party afterwards."

"That's okay," Lowell said. As soon as he had possession of the phone, he immediately snapped it in half.

"Hey, what are you doing? What did you do that for?" Destruction of anything of value riled her.

"Can't call for Manny, can you?" Lowell taunted. "You weren't supposed to play tonight."

"Is that why you tied me up? What did that accomplish?"

"We were going to make you disappear." Lowell brushed unkempt hair from his eyes and stammered, "Just for awhile to make your CDs even more in demand. Being Christmas and all."

"You mean, the pirated CDs?" His delivery was so halting that full understanding dawned in Rebecca. Lowell was saying someone else's words. "Who's we? I know you're not doing this alone."

"Never mind." Sweat seeped from Lowell's pock marked face. "I'm not ratting on my friends."

"Well, your friends' plan didn't work." Rebecca pulled herself to her full height. Maybe if she could pretend bravado, it would work. "Now move out of my way. It's time I get back to the lobby."

"No way." He grabbed her arms and pushed her away from the door. "I'm not going to get caught and you're not telling anyone." He tried to put a hand over her mouth, but when he released her arm to do so, her arm was free to block him from doing so.

"Lowell, stop! You're not thinking clearly," she tried to reason with him, her panic rising higher and faster than when she experienced stage fright. "We've always gotten along. At least listen to me!" Since she was wiggling, he pinned her arms to her side. *When did teenage boys grow so tall?* He towered over her by six inches. Overpowering him wasn't possible. Talking him down was her only hope.

"Where are your friends now?"

"Dunno." Lowell licked his lips and looked uncertain as if he caught his first fish and didn't know what to do with it. His grip tightened.

"Tell me who talked you into this."

"I already told you. I'm not a snitch!" His body trembled.

"Lowell, look I'm trying to be your friend now." Rebecca took a leap. "You've got a record?"

"I'm not going back to juvie! Tony already called me at home tonight after the police interrogated him. I split before they got to my house."

"Lowell, you are in so much trouble right now... but you can fix this. But you've got to listen."

He shook his head no.

"Lowell. Look. Where are your friends? They're not here. And they won't be here for you later. They set you up. They used you to get access to me." She saw his body pause as if he might be listening. "Think this through.

"You can't do anything to me. People are waiting on me. Lots of people. You can't force me to go with you. If you hurt me, I can scream or at the very least, that door," Rebecca nodded her head since he still pinned her arms, "is the only way out, and there are enough witnesses to identify you."

"Just shut up!"

"Lowell. You can fix this. Let me help you fix it."

"I can't go back there!"

Rebecca noticed Lowell's eyes shine with gathering tears and softened her voice even further. "What you already did yesterday is a federal offense. Your age is on the borderline. They could charge you as an adult... and then you're going to prison. Where are your friends now? They'll let you swing on your own unless you take control of your life right this minute."

He dropped his hold on her and paced as if caged. "What am I going to do?"

"Lowell, listen to me." Rebecca pleaded, desperate to get his wandering attention again. "You have the power to make things better for yourself. Be the first to speak up and everything will go easier for you." She paused for a moment. "I'll even help you."

"How can *you* help me?"

"Turn yourself in and I'll do everything I can to push that you are processed as a minor. So will Manny. He'll help too. One year, all your records are expunged."

"What's that?"

"It means, when you turn 18, your record is sealed as if it never happened. You can get a fresh start. You mentioned a guitar. Wouldn't you rather be playing in your own band, rather than rotting in prison? To get all that, all you have to do is speak up now and turn yourself in. Obviously, someone put you up to this. Someone who *doesn't* have your best interest at heart. I know you're better than this." Rebecca watched him and prayed she uttered the right words.

Lowell stared at her and wiped his nose with his sleeve. She sensed he was wavering, so she gently pressed on. "You could be the hero in all this. You could be instrumental in helping the authorities break the counterfeiting ring. They'll probably even give you immunity if you agree to help."

"And you won't tell my dad?" he asked.

"I won't, if that's what you want. That doesn't mean he's not going to find out."

Lowell's face crumpled. "Okay, I'll do it. I'm sorry. I didn't really mean to hurt you."

Rebecca approached him and put a hand on his shoulder. "Let's go find Manny. He can help you."

Lowell stepped aside and they went to find Manny. Rebecca explained what happened briefly to her agent. He and Lowell went to the security office and the hired policemen were alerted, while Rebecca autographed CDs for her fans.

After an exhausting hour of pasting a smile on her face, and signing her name more times than she could count, Manny opened the car door as she sank into the seat.

"You didn't want to press charges?" Manny asked her.

"Tonight was about Toys for Tots, giving presents to kids whose parents don't have the resources to give them surprises. Lowell is a needy kid in an adult body. It only seemed fitting. Maybe this can help him get his life straightened out." She sighed, "it might be out of my hands though. They have multiple violations they can charge him with. All I can hope to be is a good witness to what's right about him."

"You're too good, Becky."

"And Manny?"

"Yes?"

"No more stage gigs, promise me," she

said in earnest.

"You got it, babe!" *I'll tell her about the booking in London after the holidays. She'd take it better then.* "Now no more worries," he instructed. "It's party time. Let's celebrate a Harpy Christmas!"

Copyright ©2007 Peggy Jaegly

Author Profiles

(in order of appearance)

Sue Ann Jaffarian is the author of the popular Odelia Grey mystery series, as well as the upcoming Ghost of Granny Apples series scheduled for 2009. Sue Ann lives in Los Angeles, California, and is sought after as a motivational and humorous speaker. She is an active member of Sisters In Crime and Mystery Writers of America. Visit Sue Ann on the web at **www.sueannjaffarian.com**

Earl Staggs, a Derringer Award winner, has seen his short stories published in numerous magazines and anthologies. He served as Managing Editor of *Futures Mystery Anthology Magazine* and as President of the Short Mystery Fiction Society. His mystery novel, MEMORY OF A MURDER, was published in 2005. He welcomes comments on his work at **EarlStaggs@sbcglobal.net**

Thomas H. Cook is the author of twenty-one novels. He has been nominated for the Edgar Award seven times and his novel THE CHATHAM SCHOOL AFFAIR won the Edgar for Best Novel in 1996. His various works have also been nominated for the numerous awards, including the Barry, which he won for RED LEAVES. His novel PLACES IN THE DARK won the Martin Beck Award in 2000. His short story, "Fatherhood" won the Herodotus Prize for Best Historical Mystery in 1998.

Gail Farrelly writes mystery novels, articles about the mystery field, and Op-Eds, as well as satire pieces for a British website, **www.TheSpoof.com**. Her first mystery was named to the Washington Irving Book Selection List. The latest book is CREAMED AT COMMENCEMENT: A GRADUATION MYSTERY. Gail shares a website, **www.farrellysistersonline.com**, with her sister Rita, who is also mystery writer; first chapters of the Farrelly mysteries are available on the website.

Nick Andreychuk is a Derringer Award-winning author. His stories can be found in *Crime and Suspense*, *Crimestalker Casebook*, FEDORA I & III, *Great Mystery and Suspense*, *Mouth Full of Bullets*, HARDBROILED and TECHNO-NOIR, among many other publications. Nick's work can also be found in BULLET POINTS, an upcoming anthology of short-short crime fiction that he co-edited. Readers can contact him at **nickandreychuk@hotmail.com**

Herschel Cozine's stories and poems have appeared in many of the national children's magazines. Herschel's work has also appeared in *Alfred Hitchcock Mystery Magazine*, *Ellery Queen's Mystery Magazine, Woman's World*, *Orchard Press Mysteries*, *Mouth Full Of Bullets*, *HandHeldCrime*, *Great Mystery and Suspense* and others. His e-mail address is **hcozine@yahoo.com**

Frank Zafiro has served as a police officer since 1993. Most of his stories take place in fictional River City, with recurring characters. His first River City novel, UNDER A RAGING MOON, was published in 2006. The sequel, HEROES OFTEN FAIL, was released in September 2007. Over fifty of his short stories appear in print and online magazines, as well as several different anthologies. You can keep up with him at **www.frankzafiro.com**

Chris Grabenstein is the Anthony award-winning author of the John Ceepak/Jersey Shore mysteries TILT A WHIRL, MAD MOUSE, and WHACK A MOLE plus the holiday thrillers SLAY RIDE and HELL FOR THE HOLIDAYS. In 1986, he and his college buddy Ronny Venable wrote THE CHRISTMAS GIFT starring John Denver for CBS TV and it still shows up every holiday season on cable TV. You can visit Chris on the web at **www.ChrisGrabenstein.com**

Deborah Elliott-Upton's published credits include *Writer's Digest*, *Great Britain's Fiction Feast*, *Millennium Science Fiction and Fantasy*, *Beginnings*, *Mystery Reader's Journal* and business trade magazines. A past book reviewer for the *Amarillo-Globe News*, the internationally-published author teaches Writing & Marketing the Short Story online and at the college level. Five of her short stories were optioned for opening episodes of a proposed television series. A weekly columnist at **www.criminalbrief.com** , she can be reached at **www.expressedimagination.com**

Jan Christensen has had over forty short stories published. Some are available on-line in either current issues or the archives of *Crime and Suspense*, *Hardluck Stories*, *Mysterical-e*, and *Nefarious*. Her first novel, SARA'S SEARCH, was published in 2004, and she's working on two more, plus another dozen or so short stories. More about Jan at **www.janchristensen.com**

Austin S. Camacho has written four detective novels about Hannibal Jones - Blood and Bone, Collateral Damage, The Troubleshooter, and Damaged Goods -plus two action thrillers. He's active in several writers' organizations and teaches writing at Anne Arundel Community College. To pay the mortgage he answers media queries for the Defense Department. Camacho lives in Springfield, Virginia with his wife Denise and Princess the Wonder Cat. Learn more at **www.hannibaljonesmysteries.com**

Tony Burton is the author of the Rev. Thomas Wilson mystery series and the editor of the Crime and Suspense ezine. Over 150 of Tony's short stories and articles have appeared in newspapers, anthologies and various online and print venues. Tony is a member of the Sisters In Crime, and lives in northwest Georgia with his lovely wife Lara, where he writes, publishes and teaches writing at the Harris Arts Center. Visit him at **www.tonyburton.biz**

Gay Toltl Kinman has eight award nominations (including Agathas) for her writing. She has short stories published in American and English magazines, over one hundred and fifty published articles, six children's books, a young adult mystery, two adult mysteries and six short plays produced. Gay also co-edited a cookbook and a book promotion publication, writes book review columns for two writing magazines and teaches writing. Gay has library degree and law degrees. Keep up with her at **www.gaykinman.com**

Margaret Fenton is a life-long mystery fan, social worker, and writer. She has finished her first full-length amateur sleuth manuscript and enjoys writing short stories. Margaret was nominated for the Mark Austin Segura Award in 2007. She coordinates the annual mystery fan conference, Murder in the Magic City, in Birmingham, Alabama. She currently serves as president of her local Sisters in Crime chapter. To learn more, visit **www.margaretfenton.com**

Peggy Jaegly keeps her hands busy with writing and creating beautiful music on her seven harps. She keeps hoping to meet someone like Manny in real life. Visit her at **www.therightnote.us** to learn more about her CDs, books and services.

Printed in the United States
131013LV00007B/40/A